LEAVE THE LIGHT ON

A Paranormal Romance

India Vane

INDIA VANE BOOKS

For the gothic romantics who dream of wearing a white nightgown
and curling your finger through a brass candlestick holder as you walk
through a haunted house bathed in moonlight...

For the readers who hear "I have crossed oceans of time to find you"
and melt...

For the lovers who swear to find each other in every lifetime...

And for the lost souls who never stop seeking the light...

...this one is for all of you.

Playlist

The list below contains just a few of the songs that accompany scenes. Find the full "Leave the Light On" Playlist on Spotify with the code.

- "Once Upon a Dream" – Lana Del Rey

- "Salvatore Orchestral Cover" – Robbie Devine

- "As the World Caves In" – Sarah Cothran

- "Middle of the Night" (Violin) – Joel Sunny, Dramatic Violin

- "Can't Help Falling In Love" (Dark) – Tommee Profitt, brooke

- "Solas" – Jamie Duffy

- "The Secret History" – Kerry Muzzey, Andrew Skeet, The Chamber Orchestra of London

- "Spiegel im spiegel" – Arvo Part, Angele Dubeau, La Pieta

- "Silhouette" – Aquilo

- "I Found" – Amber Run

- "Sirens" – Fleurie

- "There's a Ghost" – Fleurie

- "Arrival of the Birds" – The Cinematic Orchestra, London Metropolitan Orchestra

- "Bones" – MS MR

- "The Woods" – Hollow Coves

- "Barbara Allen" (Traditional) – The King's Singers

"The sea, once it casts its spell, holds one in its net of wonder forever."

Jacques Yves Cousteau

"You best start believing in ghost stories, Miss Turner. You're in one."

Captain Barbossa, Pirates of the Caribbean

PROLOGUE

1791

The sea is as unforgiving as the past. Angry, dark waves rise and fall, rocking and tossing the ship as though it was driftwood in the vastness of the water. The black clouds that began as an imminent creeping ooze in the gray sky have slicked the world in a hopeless color that holds no space for light. Even the wind for our sails betray our course, whipping through the material and rigging with such spiraling fervor that it could fiercely uproot a strong oak tree. And I, quartermaster to this vessel, stand as a sentinel in the face of a battle that threatens to tear us apart.

Below deck, a single lantern remains, swinging with wild abandon and holding to its rusted hook with only a prayer, as no other effort could be spared for it. The remainder of the crew have devoted their strength and attention to the creaking timber of the hull and the lack of stability in the unsecured cargo aboard that have begun crashing about. The shouts and calls that were once determined and steadfast, now carry only desperation, stripped of all command. When the storm had begun its creeping trek toward the ship, we had prepared. But now as its biblical wrath rains down upon us, there is no course left but to fight to survive it.

Against the blackest of nights and the cruelty of the storm, my resolve remains steadfast and loyal to her. Always to her. My darling light. When the lightning crashes and the ship is knocked sharply to starboard, I clutch the gold ring in my breast pocket to steady and ground me, body and soul. My other hand grasps at the slick rail as I fight to maintain my bearings through the wind and rain. Listening for the captain's calls over the devilish howling of the gales, I push my way forward to ensure his orders are being carried out by the crew below.

"Clear the deck! Secure the rigging! Batten the hatches!" the captain bellows, his voice cracking as he strains over the sheer volume of the chaos. The thunder rolls like an undercurrent beneath his commands like the ancient gods that once owned this world before us. What was once a booming voice is barely a whisper now, devoured by the same tempest that threatens to consume our ship whole. But alas, amidst the menacing frenzy of it all, I hear it. It's beautiful, the faintest of melodies in the back of my mind.

"Mast!" Collins screams before the sound of his cry is interrupted by the sickening crack of the heavy wood onto the deck, crashing down like the gavel of god himself on the day of reckoning. Its weight and severity crushes him, and throws three others into the dark ravenous waters that surround us.

As several of our crew scramble to cut it loose, I already know the coldness of the truth. I can feel the result of its damage before they report it.

Alas, the melody finds me again. It's faint, but haunting in its unsuspecting persistence. I faintly recall humming it aloud just this morning, or did I whistle it? Heavens, I know better than to whistle on board, yet if love hath clouded my judgement and made it possible for me to bring ill fortune to this endeavor with my foolishness and longing...

Before I can summon the wishful urge or hope of the guiding beacon, the swinging mast strikes me hard in the chest. I'm flung from my post on the deck, and thrown down into the unruly depths below.

When my shattered form hits the water, the frigid cold wraps me in an immediate and merciless embrace. I am enveloped in total darkness like death's shroud save for one glimmer in the abyss - the memory I cling to of the light in her eyes when she promised me her hand. My legs fight, kicking about instinctively to keep me afloat, warring for the refuge of the surface. I breathe half sea air, half sea itself, choking and gasping as I'm dragged back under again and again.

Her melody seeps into my mind as I reach the peaceful edge of acceptance. It sings that although my love may be undying, this mortal form is no match for Poseidon's fury. As I grasp my breast pocket once more and curl my trembling fingers around the ring, I will my final breath to carry the oath I will never get the pleasure to speak to her - the one meant for her when we anchored in England. Gasping for breath, I seal my eyes shut tightly against the water I know I cannot fight. I call forth the vision of the place I dreamed we would live. A cough brings sea water into my tired lungs, but I refuse to let go of the dream. I speak it through shivering lips and chattering teeth, using the last flicker of strength in my chest to rage against the sea for one more moment.

"I will find you again, my Nora. I will marry you and we will have the life I vowed to give you...I will restlessly and eternally search for your light until I find you once more."

I swear it and whisper it in my mind, committing it to truth. I swear it over and over until the storm takes the last breath from my lungs, and I surrender my soul to the tempest.

CHAPTER ONE

ODESSA

"**M**arcus *again*?" Aly asks me wide-eyed as I put my phone on silent and throw it in my purse with an exhausted nod of admission. "How many calls is that since we've been here?"

I open my mouth to answer, but pause when Kaya, our server, returns with three steaming plates of pasta and a refill on the bottomless garlic breadsticks for the table. Going through a nasty split with Marcus is awful, but being the third wheel to my favorite couple in the world at the coziest Italian restaurant in town lessens the looming dread a little.

"Dess, he's spiraling," Savannah warns while we all spin our forks on our plates in unison.

My attention drifts toward their hands. They're both opposite me in the small booth, and you'd think they were newlyweds with the way they remain physically linked in some way. Even through the most mindless movements like twirling spaghetti noodles, they've made it another subtle display of being utterly insync. They share a glance at her words, and I can't help but feel that this is some sort of sneaky intervention.

"He'll get over it," I offer with a shrug through a bite of spaghetti almost the size of a golf ball. "He has to, right?"

"It's been four days. He's already blown up your phone and literally every app you have. It's like he's not even listening to you say it's over. We…we don't want him to get any worse, you know?" Aly explains slowly like she's worried I could take it the wrong way and storm out. Even if I was actually mad, I couldn't be pried away from Cimino's garlic bread for anything, including the robot apocalypse.

"Aly's right, babe. Here, give me your phone. Let's just block his cheating ass right now," Savannah says, holding her palm open expectantly so I know it's a demand and not a gentle, passive suggestion.

I momentarily wince at the unwelcome casual reminder of his infidelity, the image of his graphic texts and photos still etched in my memory. I wish I could say I was one of those women who'd experienced week-long bouts of intuitive gut feelings that urged me to investigate, but unfortunately I can't. Seeing his messages had been completely by accident, and never would I have expected that, or any, type of betrayal from him. Reading the racy words and seeing the nude photos exchanged with two other women, who didn't even look to be over 21 years old, flipped an instant switch in my heart. I had instantly accepted that I was done. The person I thought I knew for years ceased to exist to me. We became strangers in less than a minute.

I reach in my purse to absently pat around the unnecessary amount of lip products and unintentionally collected logoed pens until I find my phone. As soon as I pull it out, the lock screen illuminates, displaying my Pacman background and the notification banner for the three missed calls and seven texts he's left me over the course of thirty minutes. I know Aly and Savannah can see it too, but I impulsively swipe to read them out of curiosity.

babygirl please pick up

I fucked up ok?

don't throw away 2yrs and our future bc of one stupid mistake

Dess come on ur blowing this outta proportion. It was only texting

just talk to me. We can fix this

pick up my calls

I'm sorry I'm not perfect like you. I made a mistake and ur acting like youve never done anything wrong. I deserve another chance. U owe it to us. I can't be w o you anymore.

"Holy shit, babe," Savannah remarks as she shares a disgusted look with Aly at the desperation and gaslighting threaded sloppily into the web of his impulsive words. She holds my phone in her hands, giving me a sympathetic look when she sees the texts for herself. Tapping my screen a few times with her light blue short nails, she hands my phone back to me with an expression of justice and accomplishment. "There. Blocked."

I know I should have done it myself, but I exhale a genuine sigh of relief at the weight she lifted from my tired shoulders. I knew it would feel lighter, but knowing Marcus can't call or text me feels both good and a little scary at the same time. I hope he takes the several hints to leave me alone because the damage he caused is irreversible, but there's a sharp, anxious stitch in my side that whispers darker worries.

Is this going to make him try harder or will he just give up? Doesn't he realize it's over? What if he won't let me go?

"How are you enjoying everything?" Kaya asks, interrupting my thoughts. Before I can answer, Aly chimes in with a delightfully devious expression that tells me exactly what she'll say before the order leaves her red-stained lips.

"Love it, but you know, we need a round of sambuca shots because our best friend is hella single now," she sings as Kaya smiles. "His loss, look at how perfect she is! She's going for her masters and he's just a Temu master manipulator."

Kaya looks onto me with sympathy, and I can feel the warm unspoken camaraderie between scorned women. "Men are trash. You're too good for him, I can tell. Let me get you those shots," she says with a nod, her blonde bob bouncing as she walks over to the bar to place our order.

The one silver lining of my relationship disintegrating without warning is the sudden support from female strangers. It's both heartbreaking and heartwarming to know that we've all been through it, but that we'll also help each other through the epidemic of disappointing men who aren't written by women.

After a few shots, the warmth of the sambuca makes the music sound like what I imagine it would feel like to be delicately wrapped in velvet. I feel far away from the memory of Marcus, and with the amount of pasta, breadsticks, and trauma, I'm officially ready for a nap.

When I glance at Aly and Savannah, I can't help but smile softly to myself. They look like hope. I'm not rushing to jump into another relationship, or even entertain the idea of dating anytime soon, but when I do, I wish with all my heart I find something like they have. I want to look into someone's eyes and see our future in the reflection. I want to hear the sound of their voice and be pleasantly surprised at how it soothes my spirit even on my worst day. And more than anything, I want to feel forever in their fingertips when they touch me.

Wow, I'm one sappy fucking lush.

The hour we stayed at Cimino's after the last breadstick was gone filled my cup with laughter, inside jokes, and the unmatched bond of chosen sisters. I don't typically drink, but it felt appropriate tonight, even if I was the only one. If not when your relationship falls apart and you're eating carbs with your best friends, then when, right? I was relieved when Aly offered a ride back to my apartment so I wouldn't have to sit in a rideshare. Folding a twenty, I slip it under the corner of the glass of water I drank to help offset the alcohol and slide out of the booth.

Another fun perk of having Aly and Savannah as my pseudo family? They know me enough to choose the tunes without even having to offer me the aux. We haven't even traveled one mile from Cimino's, and with the window lowered halfway, the "caraoke" as they call it, has begun. As the first verse starts to "Wannabe" by the Spice Girls, the three of us jump right into our normal routine of singing every part complete with hand movements. When we pull into the drop off zone at the front of my building, I almost don't want to puncture this pop icon bubble I've sheltered in on the way home. Who would want to go back to regular everyday life after you've experienced being a Spice Girl?

"Ugh, thank you both so much. I needed that," I say with genuine gratitude as I slip out of the car and lazily sling my purse over my shoulder.

"Anything you need, babe, you let us know. We fucking love you, ok?" Savannah replies with a smile. Aly blows a kiss to me from the driver's window and I can't imagine what I'd do through this ordeal without having them by my side. "Seriously though, if that asshole does anything else, you call us immediately."

"Love you both too and I pinky promise. Thank you again," I answer and turn to swipe my key fob at the door to open it. I look back one more time to wave at my favorite couple aside from my parents and watch as they drive on.

Opening the heavy door to the entrance, I pause, unable to shake the prickling feeling of being watched. Even with the alcohol leaving my system, I can't deny that my senses are a little off. I hurry inside and quickly pull the door shut behind me, the same way I used to do with the basement door as a kid. The odd feeling slightly subsides as soon as there's a locked door in between me and whatever imaginary monster lurks outside.

Taking a deep breath, I turn to stop by the mailboxes, happy to tick that off of my mental to do list for the day. If I don't follow through with some of these seemingly mundane tasks daily, it'll keep me up all night thinking about it. As I twist the little brass key and pull open the square slot door, I audibly sigh at the darkened empty space. With a crease of my brows, I shake my head at my own absurd intrusive thoughts. *See?* I think to myself. *There's nothing there.*

This is easily one of the only moments I'm truly thankful that Marcus and I didn't move in together. We had been touring places since my apartment is too small for both of us and he was still living with two other roommates, but we hadn't settled on one that felt just right. It always bothered me that he didn't seem to be in a hurry to get a better job or move out of his place, but knowing what I know now, it all makes sense as to why he dragged his feet. It also stands to further my mom's theory that everything happens for a reason, and that what's meant to find me will find me. She's always been an intuitive and empathic soul, which makes her words of wisdom like medicine for my heart in times like this.

Walking up the stairs to the third floor, I start to feel the exhaustion pull at my already heavy eyelids and weary muscles. I can't wait to cuddle up with Mildred, the cutest little chubby Calico that ever lived. Aside from my best friends, Mildred is a certified secret keeper since apparently I talk to myself out loud more than I realized. Reaching the second floor, I will my body to give me the last boost of energy I store in my reserves so I can drag my belly full of carbs into my bed and try to sleep off the emotions I'm still struggling to compartmentalize. All I've sorted out so far is that Marcus cheated on me repeatedly, I don't have the desire to date anymore, and instead of being angry, I'm just numb and over it.

Reaching the top of the stairs, I freeze in my spot and my mind stops processing instantly when I see it. Toward the end of the hall on the left where my welcome mat sits, there is an unmistakably red floral arrangement waiting for me. I glance to the other doors, and an eerie silence hangs heavily in the air as I slowly approach the unwelcome gift, like it could detonate at any moment. Standing in front of my door, I bend down carefully to pick up the small folded piece of paper jammed chaotically and carelessly between the delicate petals.

Hearing the sound of footsteps on the metal stairs I just came up, I crinkle the paper in my clammy palm and quickly enter my apartment, turning the lock on the doorknob behind me. Twisting the deadbolt and pulling the chain lock into place, I put my hands on either side of the peephole and hold my breath while I stare. Mildred must sense my anxious apprehension as she walks a figure eight between my legs to reassure me with her presence. It works a little, but the full body wave of relief settles in when I realize who the owner of the footsteps is. Frederick, the elderly man that lives across the hall who mostly keeps to himself (unless of course you ask him about boxing) fumbles with his keys to open his door. He may not look it, but the golden glove necklace around his neck tells the story of a champion in the ring.

Stepping back from the door, I toss my purse on the kitchen island and will myself to open the now damp paper in my hand. As I look down at what is no doubt Marcus' rushed handwriting on a ripped piece of an envelope, I can't do anything to fight the wave of unease that travels like an electric current through my entire nervous system. Anxiety drying my mouth, I squint at the words over and over, trying my best to wish them away. When I squeeze my eyes closed and re-open them, his words don't disappear and neither does the pit in my stomach.

Dess, I'll die without you.

CHAPTER TWO

ODESSA

"Are we feeling like it's time for that famous tiramisu you saw on the menu?" I ask the young couple at the corner table. I can tell they've been watching the prices pile up, but for whatever occasion they're celebrating, it's not about the money. Her copper hair is curled and finger-brushed to a delicate perfection and his blue eyes might as well have hearts in them. She's clearly out of his league, but I find myself thinking that about most men in relationships anymore. With a slight nod from her, I head back to the kitchen to put the order in for their dessert.

It's only been a day since I tossed that floral monstrosity in the dumpster behind my building, since I didn't want the bad vibes in my sanctuary, plus every time Mildred sees plants, she eats them and pukes little piles of shredded leaves all over the apartment. It took almost twenty minutes for Aly and Savannah to stop lecturing me this morning about not calling them and reporting it right away. They told me to call the police, but I haven't yet. Nothing else has happened, and I think he might be getting the hint finally. I'm scared that if I call and he's on the verge of backing off, he'll be enraged at the police report and it'll get worse. The best thing I've convinced myself I can do is ignore him and keep my normal routine. I couldn't even keep his attention in our relationship, so I doubt he'll stay hot on my trail now that he's free to pursue whatever barely legal interests he has.

I just wish I wasn't so on edge tonight. It's my first shift since the breakup and thanks to Marcus posting our business for sympathy on every app a week ago, almost every server, line cook, and valet knows I'm single. It's not that I mind, but I hate that he wasn't as open about why it all fell apart. I don't care if everyone thinks I broke his heart out of nowhere for no good reason, but it's the lack of accountability and desperate need to crowdsource sympathy and support that gets under my skin. Every once in a while, I hear his name or mine in the whispers of the staff in our blind spots where we stand to vent about customers and management. It's almost like high school, but this time, I can't just hide in the library and eat my lunch with my nose buried in a book about ancient Egypt.

Lifting the plate of tiramisu off the pass, I put it onto a tray with the draft beers I owe Table 12 on the way. Passing the server station, two girls give me a wordless commiserate expression and I return the straight smile head nod combo. I don't have anything else to offer anyway. I don't know how many times I can hear how sorry he is or how sorry everyone else is for me. I just want to focus all of my remaining energy on my degree and let the past be the past.

Approaching the four top table of what could only be described as human flashcards of male stereotypes, I hand gym bro and finance bro their beers while checking the refill status of red pill and football mansplainer. As I turn to deliver the tiramisu to the couple, I feel a hand touch my arm and it makes my skin immediately break out into goosebumps. It wasn't the touch itself, it was the pressure, like a set of fuzzy handcuffs. I know he didn't want to spook me, but the ease of putting hands on a woman is never a green flag. I hold the dessert in my hand, locking eyes with finance bro and I'm not sure what my gaze communicated, but he raises his hands in a mock surrender signaling that my reaction was somehow dramatically overstated.

"Whoa there, chill I just had a question," he says with a nonchalant chuckle, the hardened gel in his blonde hair reflecting the low light above their table.

"Sure, what can I help you with?" I ask, maintaining my customer service voice that we all learn on the first day of any service industry job. His slimy smile makes my insides knot and I can't put my finger on why he seems like a scumbag, but I guess the mental nickname I gave him should be enough explanation.

"We were just wondering if it was you. You're Odessa, right? Marcus' ex?"

The moment the last word seeps out of his tragically thin lips, I feel the boulder in my stomach turn. The four guys look to me expectantly, and although I'm sure it's just out of curiosity, I can't escape the unease that's cementing my rubber-soled shoes to the floor. Just when I open my mouth, the stern maitre d' approaches to move me along to the table so the ice cream accompanying the tiramisu doesn't melt any faster. Her eyes assess me through her glasses and she curtly nods, another unspoken conversation between women where I don't have to put voice to the way I feel. As I scurry away to the corner table to deliver the dessert, I can hear her asking if there's anything else they need before she delivers their check.

No one questions me as I hide in the back until the guys leave, and I'm thankful for it. Even in my 30s, I still don't know why there isn't a handbook on how breakups are supposed to work, but damn would it make me feel more comfortable right now. The clearer boundaries are, the safer I feel and this is definitely making me feel like I want to spiral. I swear I've seen Marcus' face a few times outside the windows tonight, and although I know my stress is manifesting itself, that table was too much. Maybe I came back to work too early.

When Clara, the maitre d' and my personal savior for the night, comes back to where I've hunkered down with a comfort bread roll, she tells me that they've just left so I'm free to pick up the check and buss the table. I thank her with a nod and remind myself to set aside some of their tips for her, if they've even left one. It's usually the finance bros that convince themselves and the table that tipping is a scam to overcharge. *If you're cheap, just say that.*

I walk back over to their table, relieved that it's finally empty, and how much lighter the atmosphere is without their scrutinizing stares and whispers. They've picked at their food and drinks, not finishing anything and it's like they weren't even here tonight to eat. *No. Stop thinking like that. You're being paranoid,* I reassure myself. Picking up the little black folder, I can feel the thick bulge inside and I'm hoping at least the tip isn't just as much a stereotype as they were. I offer a smile to Raf, the busser that shares my love for reading, and walk back to the server station to close out their tab.

As I enter my four digit code into the register, two things happen at once. I open the small black check holder to see the bill signed out and a cash tip...along with a note on the back of the customer copy that's wrapped around the bills that I can't tear my eyes away from.

He deserves another chance.

I read the words as Clara comes to find me and as much as I don't want it to be true, I know the vase of roses in her hands are for me. She looks just as uncomfortable holding them as I do knowing full well who they're from. My suspicions are confirmed when I see the small card, and my eyes rim with tears as she puts them immediately in the trashcan next to me on top of the food scraped from plates over the past hour.

I can't live without you.

"Honey, I think you should go home. Raf and the girls can finish up the last few tables, ok?" Clara offers with a soft smile and slight concern around the corners of her brown eyes. I would have argued or lied and said that I was fine to finish my shift, but if I'm being honest with myself, I really just want to crawl back into bed with Mildred and erase this from my memory - that is, after I call the police to file a report. Aly and Sav were right.

I nod as Clara puts a wrinkled hand on my back to rub maternal reassurance into my tired frame. Watching her approach the other girls, I grab my purse out of the locker and leave the generous tip on the counter with a note for Clara and Raf to split it. I don't even want to put it in my wallet. They can keep it for covering my closing tasks and letting me take off early. Maybe I can work on my final project to close out my masters program with the extra time I'll have tonight. Or maybe I'll just binge more history documentaries in my pajamas.

Thinking about the choices, I walk to the employee parking in the alley down the street from Desert Oasis, the only restaurant I've ever liked the management of. As I get within eyeshot of my green Honda Civic, I am suddenly hyper aware of my surroundings. The world seems too quiet and the air seems still and heavy. I quicken my pace to one level below fully breaking out into a run, and when I reach my door, I feel like I'm lifting my legs out of the water right as a shark snaps its jaws closed to pull me back under.

Fumbling with my key fob as my hands shake, my purse slides off my shoulder and I drop my keys. Swearing to myself and fighting the skin-prickling sensation of being watched, I try to act calm and unsuspecting as I wrap my fingers around them. The sound of heavy quickened steps rush me as I snap straight up coming face to face with Marcus as he grabs my upper arm with force, the smell of tequila wafting off of him like cologne.

CHAPTER THREE

ODESSA

I feel every bit of Marcus' fingertips pushing into the skin of my upper arm as he yanks me away from my car, from my escape, and I freeze when I see his face. His usual clean-shaven face is peppered with uneven facial hair and there's a red rim around his eyes that could either be from crying or an alcohol-induced irregular sleep schedule. The way he's walking and talking indicates the latter. He must still be drunk.

"You b-blocked my calls," he slurs with a menacing sneer, as if to insinuate that it is against some rule I don't know about. I open my mouth to speak, but before I can, he tries to lean in and kiss me. When I recoil, the insult to his gesture twists his features and his crescendoing belligerent aura results in the grip on my arm tightening even more like a hungry boa constrictor.

"Marcus, stop," I say with as much strength as I can, my own version of camouflage to hide the sheer terror and panic threatening to lock my limbs before I get the chance to run. Even when he's like this, he knows me enough to know I'm not as brave as I wish I was.

"Give me another chance, baby. You're my girl. You'll always be my girl, Dess, no matter *what*."

His words elicit a physical response from me the moment he speaks, and the nausea isn't just from that, it's the smell of him. This can't be the man I committed myself to for years. At first, my instinct is to reason with him, but when I raise my eyes to meet his, I don't see Marcus in there anymore. I see a desperate, drunk cheater who is quickly graduating to an abusive narcissist, and I decide on my plan of action faster than my anxiety can talk me out of it.

"Help!" I cry as I swing my other arm around to meet his face. Before he can react, my nails dig lines down the side of his face from just above his eyebrow down to the middle of his cheek. His bracing hold on my arm is gone in less than a second, and I don't miss a single minute of the slim chance I've given myself. As he covers his face, I click the key fob to unlock my door and I jump in as fast as I can, locking it behind me only a moment before he roughly wrenches the door handle.

"Open the fucking door," Marcus shouts, hitting the window with his damp palms when he realizes I locked him out and he can't reach me anymore.

My hands shake and my heart pounds mercilessly against my rib cage as I finally get the key in the ignition and turn it. With the fresh scratches on his cheek, Marcus rests his forehead onto my window, and I can hear him through the glass as I throw the car into drive.

"You can't keep running away from me," he says, the sinister words juxtaposed by the softness in his tone. It's the last thing I hear before I step on the gas so suddenly the car jolts forward, throwing off his balance.

The mindless autopilot drive to Aly and Savannah's house goes by in a flash, and when I park, I don't even remember anything about the ride. It's almost as if I blinked and the next minute, I was here. At the sound of the car in the driveway, Aly opens the door to look outside and the second she sees me step out, she yells to Savannah to call the police. Rushing over to me, I fall apart in her arms and sob as her eyes take me in from my pale face, to the bruising on my arm, to the way I'm holding my hand. With Aly's hold around my shoulders, I let her lead me into their living room and cover me with a blanket when I wordlessly sink into the couch.

I'm a little more coherent when the police arrive, which helps when I have to recount my story a few times and let them take pictures of my hand and arm. I update them on everything leading up to tonight and even hand over my phone at Savannah's idea to help in establishing his increasingly threatening behavior. When they recommend filing a restraining order, all I can do is nod my head in favor of the paper that might grant me a little bit more security and peace of mind - assuming he'll follow it. They give me a lot of information about pressing charges and more, but I'm not able to retain anything. I'm so tired and overwhelmed, I just want to sleep for ten years.

Aly and Savannah thank the two officers as they leave the house, and I'm left with the desire to cry, sleep, and throw up all at the same time. It already feels unreal, or that my encounter with him happened a month ago from the amount of disassociation I've already started to allow to settle in.

"Dess?" Aly says softly as she pats the top of my hand, sitting on the couch next to me. I look up to meet her eyes, but fail to utter a word. "I called your parents, ok? They want you to check in before you go to sleep. Here's my phone, just push call."

I tap the screen without thinking, the idea of my mom and dad's voices wrapping around me like a long distance hug offers the promise of comfort a girl can only get from her parents. The call doesn't even last one full ring before my mom picks up.

"Honey, are you ok?" she asks anxiously like any mother would, and it instantly makes me want to sob all over again. I feel Savannah's head on my shoulder and Aly's hand on my back as I talk to my mom.

"I-I'm better now," I answer honestly.

"Aly and Savannah told us everything, sweetheart. He's already contacted us tonight about trying to help make us all a family again, so we filed a restraining order too," she reports. The deep guilt consumes more of me at her words, and the tears start building again.

"I'm so sorry, Mom," I offer, mortified that I can maintain a high GPA in my masters program, but can't spot my own boyfriend cheating on me for who knows how long. Before that train of thought is allowed to travel any farther down the tracks, she stops me.

"Honey, no. A man's terrible behavior is his own fault, well, and maybe his mother's for raising such a loser," Mom suggests. The side of my lips curl up at her comedic wisdom, reminding me of yet another reason why my mom is one of my best friends. I can hear my dad shouting to her in the background and she clears her throat before continuing. "Your dad and I want you to come stay out here with us while this blows over, ok?"

"At the lighthouse?" I ask with a puzzled look. By the hopeful way Aly and Savannah are watching me, my mom must have already shared the plan with them.

"Yes, on Corlucius Island. Dad and I are still filming and working on the cleanup before we can renovate, so why don't you just take some time off from the restaurant for the summer. You can work on your project here while you help us out. There's an extra bedroom in the keeper's house, so there's plenty of room."

I open my mouth to tell her I'll think about it, but it's then that I realize there's not really anything to consider. I could have Aly and Savannah babysit Mildred since she hates to fly, and I could get out of the area and truly give my project my full attention which I don't think I'll be able to give here if I'm always on edge. I can't seem to find any negatives, and it's a slow season when the summers get so hot here anyway.

"Ok," I agree. I don't miss the shared look of relief my best friends give each other over my head while I listen to my mother gush over the phone about how excited she and Dad are to have me help. "I've always wanted to see Massachusetts."

While Aly and her type A personality handle my travel arrangements for the morning, and Mildred's care plan while she stays at her home away from home, Savannah helps me pack what I'll need for the summer. Neither one of them wanted me to be alone at my apartment, and honestly, I didn't like the idea of it either, so I enjoyed their company while we packed and ended the night with a sleepover that doubled as an impromptu goodbye party and a house cleansing. Something tells me there's not enough sage in this apartment to wipe away the curse of Marcus Netterman.

CHAPTER FOUR

ODESSA

"Thanks for tuning in to this week's episode of Destination Restoration with Dave and Becca! We'll see you next Thursday for-" my mother's voice abruptly cuts off as I press next on the playlist they have on their channel. I've been meaning to catch up on their videos, and this flight is the perfect time, especially since I was spontaneously upgraded which I'm convinced is somehow their doing.

Not only am I enjoying the perks of a business class seat for the first time ever, I'm also experiencing a full reset on all of my social media platforms. Aly and Savannah were right. Knowing that Marcus' number is blocked and there's a restraining order is comforting, but deactivating my Instagram and Tiktok accounts feels so freeing. The anxiety I felt with every vibration of my phone is nonexistent as I adjust my posture in the most comfortable airline seat I've ever felt, and sip the Bloody Mary that Chelsea, the sweetest flight attendant, recommended.

I smile as the intro music to Destination Restoration filters through my airpods, and I can't help but be proud of what they've built and the example they set for me. Growing up, it was a lot to handle with them always off and on new projects, plus editing all of their content, but seeing how it's paid off and what it's allowed them to do is admirable. I didn't realize it when I was younger, but now that I'm looking back through more mature eyes, they were lucky enough to combine their passions and create a brand and business together. While all of my other friends' parents were cycling through divorces, affairs, or blowout fights, my parents were working together on a shared dream that kept them fighting for each other.

Finishing the last video that detailed their move from Southern California to New England, which was hilarious to watch them adjust to the weather, I am finally caught up to the most recent ones where they talk about the process and decision to purchase their first historical landmark property - The Corlucius Lighthouse. At first, I wasn't sure what would entice my cautious parents to suddenly uproot their entire lives to move across the country to restore this particular property, but the second the camera focused on the island and the lighthouse came into view, I felt it. I've seen lighthouses in movies and in photos, but something about this lighthouse is so alluring. It calls to you.

"Welcome to Corlucius Island, home of The Corlucius Lighthouse. As you can see, Dave and I had to ferry here. We'll be settling in and making weekly visits to town where we'll most likely have to upload our videos in the cafe since the internet speed on the island is pretty shoddy," my mom begins.

"Lucky for me, that means Becca can't access any online shopping so I can experience life without daily deliveries," Dad teases. She smiles and playfully rolls her eyes.

"Don't let him fool you, friends. Every time a package comes, he gets excited and asks if I ordered him a surprise," she says with a smirk as he puts an arm around her, shrugging to the camera in agreement.

"She's right, as usual. She was also right about buying this property. We weren't originally planning on making a drastic move like this until we were older, but when Becca showed me the listing, we did some research on the history behind this island and the lighthouse. We felt destined to bring it as close to its original state as possible," Dad explains.

"As you see here, come on, let's take a tour while we deep dive into the mystery of the history of The Corlucius Lighthouse," Mom begins. She's always the one that handles the storytelling for the videos, and she's great at it. Bedtime stories with Mom are one of the parts of my childhood I cherish above all others. She never read to me from a book, we would imagine the stories together and create elaborate unique adventures until I fell asleep.

I use the blanket Chelsea brought me when she did her last walk down the aisle to check on the five of us in this section, and listen to my favorite part of my parents' series. As I close my eyes, my mother's soothing voice carries through my mind, crafting the rich history of the property and all of the lighthouse keepers to date. Over and over people spent their lives making sure the guiding light burned bright through the darkness for incoming ships, allowing New England to flourish with imports and trades. I'm almost fully asleep until an idea hits me and my eyes pop open.

"Yes," I say quietly to myself in victory as I open another tab on my laptop to send a quick email to my professor. With my destructive breakup and the restraining order that followed, I was granted an extension on the deadline to announce the thesis for my project. Getting my masters in history has been all I've been focused on until Marcus turned my world upside down and shook it until all the change fell out of its pockets.

I barely pause long enough to proofread my email before pressing send, the excitement radiating through my fingertips as I click the keys in record speed. Mom and Dad were right again. The thesis I'm meant to write would come to me when it was supposed to, and I would know because it would feel like mine. They say the same thing about love and best friends, and they're never wrong. I don't know where I stand spiritually in the world, but I can't argue that the universe has always found a way to guide me to the right place at the right time, even if it's just to teach me a lesson.

The fact that I'll be able to visit with my parents, help them with their restoration, and put space between Marcus and myself all while completing the research I'll need for my project feels cosmically aligned. I send a quick text to Mom to tell her the exciting news, and another to Aly and Savannah to make them aware that I now know what it feels like to fly when you're not on a college student budget before I settle back in my seat and press play on the video again. My mother's voice resumes and my eyes drift closed, the weight of my thesis now off my mental to do list.

I didn't even realize I had fallen asleep until Chelsea softly taps my shoulder to wake me up. While it felt like nothing but a slow blink to me, my laptop battery is drained and a quick tap of my phone screen tells me it's been almost three hours. Running the back of my hand over the edges of my lips, I thank the business class gods that I didn't have drool on my face. I comb my fingers through my chestnut waves to dislodge any traces of bed head - *airline seat head?* - and start the process of ensuring I'm not holding up the line when it's time to exit.

With the slight bump from the landing gear, I text Mom to meet me at the gate and smile at the texts from Aly wishing me a productive summer and possible new career as a nepo baby influencer on my parents' show. The next incoming text makes my smile even bigger as the plane comes to a gradual full stop - a selfie of my mom and dad at the gate. Even though I just saw them a couple months ago, it feels like a bittersweet homecoming, like I'm running home after a heartbreak to be held by the people who always understand and love me unconditionally.

As I step out of the curved doorway and down the stairs, I can already feel the difference in early summer weather from Southern California's desert to the Massachusetts coastline and it's a welcome change. Shifting my bag a little higher on my shoulder, I pause as the wind whispers through my hair and draw my brows together at the slightest sensation that travels through me.

In the oddest yet briefest moment, wrapped in the delicate swirl of the gentle ocean breeze, my heart settles in my chest and I feel like I'm home after a long journey. The corner of my lips curl as I inhale a slow, deep breath of New England air, and remember my parents' wise words once more. *You are exactly where you're meant to be, at the time you're meant to be there, doing exactly what you're meant to do.* For the first time in my life, I feel that phrase take root in my soul, sprouting vines to my heart. I am exactly where I'm meant to be, at the time I'm meant to be here, doing exactly what I'm meant to do. Just as I silently move my mouth to the words in my mind, an email notification pops up on my phone.

Good Afternoon Odessa,

Thank you for submitting your unique thesis to the department. You have our approval.

Don't hesitate to reach out if you have any further questions or concerns.

Please travel safely and proceed with your research.

Thank you,

Dr. Poole

Chapter Five

Odessa

Oh my god. I should have known. I can hear my parents at the gate long before I can see them, but when I do, I feel like I'm back in middle school and they're embarrassing me in front of Brendan, my crush. From thirty feet away, I can see the neon poster boards with black paint writing, but the closer I get, the more hilariously embarrassing it becomes. Both of my parents are holding a radiation level bright green poster that says "THIS MOM IS EXCITED TO SEE HER BABYGIRL" and "THIS DAD IS EXCITED TO SEE HIS BABYGIRL"...and in the center of the poster is a hole with an arrow pointing to it, where their faces go. I'm literally walking toward two human trading cards and just like everyone else around me, I can't stop laughing.

"Wow, subtle," I say as they drop the posters and wrap me in a group hug. I might not be a kid anymore, but no matter how many candles are on my birthday cake, I'll never be too old for this. As the scent of Mom's shampoo and Dad's cigars surround me, my inner child lets a tear fall at how safe I finally feel after everything that's happened. When I'm in this brief huddle, I feel like nothing can hurt me anymore, and if someone could bottle this and sell it, they'd undoubtedly be Bruce Wayne rich.

"Come on, kiddo, did you eat lunch in the fancy first class?" Dad jests, cluing me in that they definitely did have something to do with my spontaneous upgrade. When I look up at him from behind my glasses, he smirks and throws an arm around my shoulders and the other around my mom. "Let me take the best girls out to lunch, my treat."

"You look beautiful, sweetheart," Mom whispers to me from the other side of my dad's chest, her wild golden curls bouncing as we walk. "Brilliant and beautiful." I blush at my mother's constant praise and what I've deemed as "compliment confetti" that she always sprinkles over me, especially when she knows I could use the emotional lift.

After loading my luggage into the Uber, I stare out the window as the view from my side shifts from airport parking to open road to the coziest beach town I thought only existed in Hallmark movies. When we slow to a stop in the downtown area, I'm anxiously tapping my leg in anticipation to get out and explore my new home for the next few months. The change of pace from the hustle and bustle of the desert to the leisurely stroll of Clarkston is evident as I stand next to the luggage our driver kindly unloaded on the sidewalk.

"It's like a postcard," I say without thinking while every component invades my senses until I become part of it. The smell of the ocean is still faintly present, but takes a supporting role to the scent of the warm vanilla infused in the fresh waffle cones the little diner is advertising in the window. I close my eyes to imprint it on my memory while the sounds of tourists and seagulls swirl around me. "Just so…" I trail off, trying to put the sensation into words.

"Quaint?"

"Chill?"

Both of my parents say the words at the same time and laugh at each other when we all nod in agreement. Dad picks up my bags and tips the driver while I turn to my mother to notice how she's looking at me, like she's relaxed and happy.

"I'm really happy you're here, sweetheart," she says softly, petting my hair like she used to when I was a kid. When I was younger, all I wanted to do was grow up, but now that I'm an academic and studying my ass off to eventually get my doctorate, I miss the days when my mother playing with my hair cured every bad day. Now that my brunette waves are back under her fingers, I think she still has that superpower. I'm already feeling like Marcus is a distant memory, fading just as quickly as my desire to ever wonder about calories again when food smells this good.

"Me too," I admit as Dad holds the door open. Walking into Clarkston Creamery & Deli, I can't help but take out my phone to snap a few pictures. The building is a mod podge of business endeavors from an ice cream stand to a sandwich shop to a general store to a novelty gift destination. Initially, I'm overwhelmed, but the more I take in my surroundings, it somehow completely makes sense.

We sit down at a small table near the window, the one closest to the racks of collectible shot glasses, personalized magnets, and colorful beaded keychains with little seashells at the end. The laminated menus are only one page front and back, but boast four items that are award-winning, notated by the little blue ribbon clipart. I only have a minute to peruse before an older woman who looks to be in her 70s approaches the table with a little memo pad and a pen that has a little mermaid on it.

"Hey, Sandra. We'd like you to meet our daughter, Odessa," Mom says proudly from the opposite side of the booth, looking at me with pride. When my dad joins in, I feel like a kid again showing off a macaroni noodle necklace that they parade around like the Hope Diamond. Sandra looks my way and her eyes soften, and I instantly become aware that my chronic oversharer of a mother probably already told half the town about my breakup.

"Hi, darlin'. Your mom and dad have been so excited to have you visit, they were in here just this morning gushin' about you," Sandra adds with a dimpled smile. "What can I get you?"

As we all place our orders, they take turns sharing their experience so far with the property and its restoration progress. By the time our food arrives, I'm completely up to date on all things Destination Restoration and the Corlucius Lighthouse, including their ultimate plan of flipping it for a hefty profit. Through the best order of fish and chips I've ever had in my entire life, my parents step in as my pseudo academic advisors as they share their opinions on what I could use from their research to aid me in my project. I've always loved digging through historical records, but having this jumpstart feels like fate. In between embarrassing mouthfuls of cheese-drenched french fries, I've decided to focus my efforts on the roles of the women throughout history that have participated in the keeper's duties of the island, leading also to the fruitful trade and exports that shaped Clarkston over the centuries.

With my brain going a mile a minute, I'm unable to do anything aside from use my notes app to jot down a few points to elaborate on when I get settled into whatever living arrangements I'll have. I offer to pay the tab when Sandra returns, but Dad refuses to let her take my card, making her smile and shrug at me. When I finish my last bullet point, I zip my phone back into my small purse and slide out of the booth.

As I exit the diner with a full stomach, I feel more and more like a local and I can't wait to see my parents' boat and step foot on the island. I've seen so many of their videos, I can envision the lighthouse in my mind, but actually standing at its base and looking up to the light is something I'm really looking forward to.

To my surprise, the walk from the diner to the dock is a lot shorter than I anticipated, which I celebrated in my head since I'm not that enthusiastic about physical activity after a decent meal full of cheese, starch, and fried fish. Standing on the wooden planks while Dad gets my bags loaded onto The Odyssey, I see the minute my mom gets an idea and I know what it is before she says a word. With excitement from ear to ear, she takes her digital camera out from her tote bag and flags down a fisherman that isn't actively gutting his catch.

With my mom's smile, it's a shock she didn't strive for world domination because one minute the man is fishing and the next, he's getting "all the angles" as she says. She poses us with me in the middle and both of them holding an arm over my shoulder, and then another one with all of us giving a very cringey thumbs up. After three poses, Dad clears his throat and the fisherman returns the camera to my mom so he can continue the real reason he's on the dock today.

I was slightly worried I could get seasick in that small of a boat, but halfway to the island, all I can do is feel the pull of it. I can't shake the feeling that I'm being reeled in by my heartstrings directly to the place I'm meant to be when I'm meant to be there. It's probably just the relief and safety washing over me now that I'm far away from my ex and surrounded by the people that love me most in this world, but as the lighthouse comes into view, I tear up and my skin breaks out into goosebumps, and for the life of me, I can't explain why.

CHAPTER SIX

ODESSA

U nloading everything from the boat onto the dock, I realize I brought a lot less than I thought from my old apartment, even for just a summer. There's more groceries than there are personal belongings, and it's a subtle reminder that I've prioritized my focus on my education and career over getting married and having children. It's not that I don't see it for myself one day, but I have yet to feel the earth shattering wave of fate coursing through my veins at the sheer sight of my destined dream person. If it's anything like what Aly and Savannah or my parents have, then it's completely and utterly worth however long the universe asks me to wait. All I know is that it wasn't Marcus.

With our hands full and The Odyssey carefully tied up, we walk up the small flight of wooden planked stairs to the grassy hill of Corlucis Island. I don't know if it's already the feeling of safety you get when you're in an isolated location like this, but my whole body feels at rest. There's an ease to my mind suddenly, and although it wasn't present until recently, I exhale a small sigh of peace and contentment. Pausing for a moment, I put everything I'm holding down and watch as my parents pause to see what I'm doing. Slipping off my shoes and pulling off my socks, I ground my toes into the softest grass and most tender earth I've ever felt.

"I knew you'd love it here," Dad says as he smiles at me before looking at my mom. She beams in return like she's a best friend waiting to show me something they're excited about.

As I tuck my shoes into the tote bag I'm holding with my laptop and notebook, my feet carry me toward the house on autopilot, like I've been here a thousand times before. The sight is unlike any photo or video, and even though I knew what the property looked like from their videos and Instagram posts, nothing could ever compare to the majesty of it in front of me.

Pausing twenty feet from the small white keeper's house, my eyes drift to the second floor small window as I fully surrender to the sensation of being home. Maybe it's that I haven't lived with my parents for over a decade, or maybe it's that I've seen so much of it on Destination Restoration, but either way, I can't recall the last time I felt this way.

Walking into the house, my bare feet transition from the soft grass to the hardwood flooring of the kitchen. The spot I stand in while I put down everything except my tote bag is warm, a ray of sunlight beaming directly onto it, and I wiggle my toes, noticing the slight chip of purple nail polish on my right big toe.

"I'll show you which room is yours," Mom says as she goes toward the steps, but I'm right there with her at her heels in an instant.

"Top right?" I guess out loud. *I'm right, I feel it.*

"Top right is the one," she responds with a smirk. "You really did watch all of our videos didn't you?"

I laugh with her as we both walk to the top of the stairs and turn right down the short hallway. There are only two bedrooms in this house, one on the left and then the other is on the right side of the hallway with the full bathroom at the end. The walls of the hallway are littered with photos of different generations and you can tell they weren't displayed to make the house a home, they were hung to preserve any morsel of history left as if to say "don't forget us, we were here". According to the first episode of my parents' series, the last owners found the photos during the genealogy research of former keepers, so they framed them to remember their service and in some cases, sacrifice.

Entering the bedroom, it's reminiscent of any typical old New England bed and breakfast. Against the weathered white walls, there's a small freshly made double bed on a wooden frame, the maroon blanket like open arms waiting to comfort me. There's a wooden nightstand next to the bed, a mirror on the wall, a small bookshelf with a few classics, and then I spot my favorite part. In front of the window, there's a wooden desk with a chair tucked in under it. I don't hesitate to rest my tote bag on top, removing my laptop and notebook to place them on top of their new home, which has a much better view than the one in my apartment. On the windowsill, there's a white tall candlestick in a brass holder that looks like it's been burned about ⅓ of the way down. I reach my hand out to move it, but pause. It makes my view look like a window through time with the small cracks in the pane. Continuing to reach for it, I touch the curled handle of the brass holder instead.

"Get settled in and take a shower if you want, honey, then later we'll do dinner. Your dad insists upon grilling, so come down when you smell them burning," she chuckles. Kissing me on the forehead, she turns to leave me in what will be my summer sanctuary.

Standing alone for the first time in my room next to the desk, I walk to the bed to toss my other bag. As I cross the room, the floorboards under the small patterned rug creak and the sound seems so loud in a house where there isn't the background noise of a tv or speakers. It's just quiet, but a heavy quiet that settles over in a comfortable way, like a blanket draped over you by someone who loves you when you fall asleep on the couch.

Digging through my bag on top of the bed, I pull out a camera to take a few photos for my research before setting it on the desk to record. I don't have a lot to report yet, but after learning the hard way how important content is as well as documenting everything, I turn on the camera to log my first few hours.

When my initial impressions are complete, I stretch my arms over my head as the thought of a hot shower calls to me like a lover. Thankful again for limiting the amount of luggage, and parents willing enough to carry my stuff upstairs, it doesn't take long for me to find the one with my toiletries and the other with my clothes. Carrying everything with me to the small bathroom, I start the water and surprise myself with the lack of a loud playlist in the background. I usually don't do much of anything without some sort of noise to quell the constant trains of thought rolling through my mind, but something about this place makes everything pleasantly palatable and slowed down.

By the time I throw on a cropped shirt and leggings after the shower, the faint smell of charred burgers waft through the air as soon as I open the bathroom door. Leaving my wavy brown hair to air dry, I bounce down the stairs, my mouth already watering at the smell of dinner as it gets stronger the closer I get.

Within minutes, I'm sitting at the circular oak table in the kitchen with my parents and we're all enjoying the first bites of our turkey burgers while Mom starts talking to me about my project. It's an interesting and slightly comical feeling that my parents and I are both working on different aspects of what feels like the same project. While they restore the house and lighthouse to its former glory, I'm digging through its history and impacts on the island.

We talk until darkness falls and the moonlight takes her place to reflect off of the sea. With a stomach full of burgers and fries, and a notebook page full of names my parents gave me of people to interview tomorrow to get me started, I say goodnight and walk up the stairs to my room, feeling the weight of the day heavier on my body with each step. Hopefully by the time I get through some of the names on this list, Dad will have the steps in the lighthouse repaired enough that we can finally see inside and maybe even get to the light at the top.

As I enter my room, the darkness makes me narrow my eyes for precision until they adjust. I walk toward the window to open my laptop, stepping on the loud creak of the floor under the carpet and wincing at the volume of it. When I reach the window, I curl my finger through the holder of the candle on a reflex, like I've done it a hundred times. Before I can process the strangeness of the motion, something catches my eye down on the jagged rock's edge of the island near the dock.

Standing still is a dark shadow just beyond the solar light post my parents added to the dock for safety. My body chills as I stand like a statue to stare at what looks like a man looking up into my window directly at me. Without a thought, I bring my hand to the glass to clear it from what must be steam or fog so I can get a better look, but when I do, he's no longer there. The dock is completely empty.

CHAPTER SEVEN

ODESSA

With the sun warming my cheeks beneath my tortoise shell glasses, I slip a folded twenty into Benny's rough hands as he keeps me steady while I step off of his boat. My parents already having established a decent rapport with a handful of prominent townspeople has given me a decent headstart on everything I need to accomplish in the next few weeks. Although I always appreciate the kindness and understanding my professor had in allowing me to push my project's deadline, I would truly prefer to be back on track to turn in my assignment with the rest of my class. Having it late is one more thing Marcus affected, and I want to prove to him, and to myself, that he didn't take this from me too.

Remembering a little bit of the town's layout from the videos I watched, and the recommendations my parents gave me last night, I hold the strap of my laptop bag on my shoulder and take a right from the dock toward the coffee shop. There's no way I'm going to be deep in research mode in the town's small public library records room without an iced coffee of some sort. As a creature of habit, I spent almost all four years of earning my bachelors with my signature iced frappuccino in my left hand and my notebook in my right, but I made a promise to fully immerse myself for the sake of authenticity during this project, so today, I'll try whatever the locals suggest.

In less than thirty minutes, the sun beams a little brighter and I'm on my way to the public library while I sip my vanilla bean iced coffee with caramel drizzle and I already feel like a new woman. With every gentle breeze that ruffles my chestnut curls, the subtle scent of the sea wraps around me, pulling me to it like a siren's song. The walk might seem long, but it's a welcome expedition to someone like me. I may as well be in a foreign country with the way I'm taking in everything from the architecture to the foliage because when it comes to my research, I catalog everything, even if just mentally.

The glass door to the library is heavier than I anticipated, so before I even get the chance to introduce myself to the two librarians behind the counter, I'm shoved into the entrance area by the sheer weight of it backed by the wind causing several papers fall out of my bag. Feeling like a human hurricane, I stutter through my words as I pick them up.

"Hi, umm, I'm Odessa, well, Dess. I-I'm here-"

"-David and Becca's girl! I'm Lena and this is Trudie. Your parents told us you'd be in today," she says as they both look at me with softened eyes and welcoming smiles.

"Great, thank you. It's so nice to meet you both," I reply and I genuinely mean what I say. There are kind people everywhere, but there's a different type of kind people in this New England coastal escape. They're tight knit, but not exclusive. Every person I've encountered so far makes me feel like this is a place I can not only be myself, but be safe to be myself. A slam onto the countertop jolts me out of my thoughts and to the present moment as I turn my head sideways to read the stack's spines.

"Your mom and dad gave us a good idea of what you might be looking for, so here's a start, dear. They seem so excited to have you spend the summer with them," Trudie chirps holding a yellow cup that says "Kiss the Librarian" in her wrinkled hands tipped with hot pink nail polish.

"Your mama is darling and your daddy is quite the looker. Two lovebirds. We've been watching every episode of their show they're making," Lena adds. "At first when the rumors went around that there was some famous real estate couple from California buying the lighthouse, we were all ready to protest, but when we found out they were going to restore it and document its history, well, that was A-ok with us. Honorary locals you all are now."

Thanking them for their thoughtfulness, I carry as many of the books as I can to the table near the window. Even though the library is smaller than the one I'm used to visiting at the university, the amount of records here is staggering. Lena and Trudie told me they would try to help me locate anything I may need, but it'll probably take me a few days just to get through the books they gave me today.

Page after page, I read through the diverse and rich history around the keepers assigned to maintaining the Corlucius Lighthouse beacon. After a few hours, my body begins to signal the need for a break. While my stomach growls, I massage my right wrist from the pages of notes I've written, and close my eyes to let them rest from reading. As if they could hear my stomach growl from the front desk, Lena breaks the silence.

"Dessa, you should take a break and eat some lunch, dear," Lena says in a softer shout. When I meet her eyes from across the room we're in, I return her smile and nod while I begin to pack up my things. "If you want to be a true local, you have to order lunch from the famous

McNamara's. It's a deli, but they also have ice cream for the perfect dessert."

"Well, I don't know how anything could compete with that," I respond with a laugh as I pack up my notes and copied paperwork of the day so far. "I'll be back tomorrow with a full report."

With a wave back to my two new local friends, I turn to walk down the street to McNamara's as my mind files away all of the new information I read through today. I knew a coastal town in New England would naturally hold a significant amount of history, but after reading a lot of personal stories, I decided that my project is going to focus more on those. Textbooks and documentaries can recount the facts, but with every word from the journals and newspapers I saw today alone, I could visualize it like I was there. The details are still vivid in my imagination as I hear the small bell ring when I push the door open and step inside, the smell of various lunch options making my mouth water instantly.

The grocery store is modest, but with all the essentials you could need, and the few tables next to the windows offer the perfect place to people-watch inside and outside. Eyeing the third table, a small red booth under the produce special drawn on the window with paint pens, I push up my glasses with one finger as I scan the deli menu. At this stage of stomach growling, I'm more concerned with which option is the fastest, but the moment I spot the italian hoagie, I'm sold.

I'm so focused on the absolute heaven I know this lunch will be that I almost miss the sound of a sneeze next to me. I was so lost in the idea of sliced pepperoni and salami that I didn't even register the other person standing next to me. When I turn to offer a quick blessing for his sneeze, I can't help but notice how much he reminds me of someone I can't place. When we lock eyes, I open my mouth to speak, but he goes first.

"Bless you," he says and immediately laughs when he sees my amused confusion. "I mean, thank you. Wait, you haven't-I'm sorry, I-"

"-Bless you," I offer to put him out of his socially awkward misery. He's only a few inches taller than I am, and the warmth of his adorably awkward smile wraps around me like a scarf, pulling a polite smile out of me. His voice seems so familiar, but maybe with a British accent, I may just have him confused with an audiobook narrator or Tom Hiddleston reading about math.

His smile widens and I turn back to the deli menu, and him to his phone in his hand. My stomach growls again just in time as an older gentleman behind the counter in an apron nods his head to me. I turn to the nameless sneezing man in his breezy blue button up shirt to see if he'd like to go first, since I admittedly was not aware of when he got in line or if I cut in front of him. He gestures for me to go ahead, and selfishly I ramble off my order without protest before letting him do the same, thankful for his kindness because I'm genuinely starving.

Sliding over to the pickup window with the glass bottle of Coca Cola I couldn't wait to open, my mind wanders for only a few minutes before the man with the apron hands me a sub wrapped in brown paper. Thankful the red booth is still open, I slink into the curved seat and open my notebook to jot down a few thoughts while I eat. The more I read of the copied materials I grabbed for homework, the more I can imagine what life here over the years must have looked like. I write a few notes as I mindlessly unwrap the sub, and let myself get lost in the white noise of the store.

I'm about to take my first bite of the hoagie when a throat clears next to me, pulling me from my thoughts. When I look up, it's the guy with the accent wearing a smile and holding his sub out with a shrug as he looks at mine. I crease my brows together, but before I say anything, he slips into the seat across from me, our knees brushing under the small table.

"I think you have my lunch," he nods. When I look closer at the sandwich I'm holding, I know he's right. Wrapping it back in the paper, we swap and he stays in the seat without asking if he can. Usually that would strike me as a bit odd, or dangerous considering I have an active restraining order against a man who also didn't ask permission, but I don't mind. I don't even know this guy's name yet, but I can't explain why my intuition tells me I'm not in danger with him.

Chapter Eight

Theodore

I've been to the States plenty of times for work, but this is my first client in Massachusetts, and I've vowed to my mum and sister that I'd truly experience it like a local instead of making every trip strictly business. They've blamed my work for the failure of my last two relationships, and their solution is that I allow myself a bit of leisure in my travels. Although it's only for a couple weeks, I've opted for a small local bed & breakfast over a hotel suite in the neighboring city, giving me plenty of opportunities to take photos to send them. I've only just settled in last night, and already I've gotten several recommendations from Mrs. Goodman during our initial meeting this morning.

Remembering the name of this small grocer was simple as I grew up being picked on by a bloke by the name of Oliver McNamara I only hope this lunch is better than Ollie's one-liners. There's only so many names you can call a kid for being overweight, but Oliver found them all. He wasn't so keen on me "glowing up like Neville Longbottom" as my sis so delicately put it, since he avoided me after I spent everyday day after school in the gym.

Getting in line at McNamara's, I found the chalk-written deli menu to be quite appealing...although, not as appealing as the woman standing in front of me. Her chocolate waves and those adorable glasses combined with the tote bag of unorganized papers and the way she tried to cover up the growl of her stomach, she reminded me of someone. It's not a regular occurrence for me to be taken by someone, but when it hits me that the person she reminds me of is Evie from The Mummy - the film that undoubtedly fueled my interest in antiques and appraising pieces of history - I can't help but take a small step closer to her.

I don't know what does it, but the moment I'm within a few feet of her, the gods curse my luck and instead of saying something, I damn near sneeze on her. *Bollocks.* And to make matters quite worse, I blessed myself instead of letting her say it first. In the classics, the woman usually renders the gentleman speechless. I only wish she would have done the same so I could preserve my dignity, but here I am speaking out of turn and with no sense at all. *Double bollocks.*

As I stand there cursing the universe for making me appear utterly dim-witted and crushing my one chance at talking to this modern day little Evie, I open my sub to realize it's not mine. I can't say for certain that the man behind the counter isn't doing his part to help me rewrite a meet cute, but either way, I'm holding her long awaited lunch and I'm moving over to her booth. Luckily, I arrive in time to save my lunch from her grasp. The moment she realizes it, she blushes, her embarrassment painting the apples of her cheeks in a shade of pink that reminds me of my mother's rose garden.

"I didn't take a bite of it. I swear," the delightful little librarian-looking darling says with a chuckle, holding her hands up in surrender, and I can't help but laugh. We trade subs, and I fight the urge to give her her space. To my surprise, she lets me stay. "I'm Odessa, but everyone just calls me Dessa."

"Theo, short for Theodore, as in my mother just adored those little chipmunks on the telly when she was pregnant," I admit shamelessly while taking a large bite out of the leafy sub in my hands. Dessa takes a bite of hers, struggling to hide her grin, but I catch the familiar curl of her beautiful lips like I've seen it a thousand times before. Maybe her resemblance to Rachel Weiz is what's giving me deja vu.

"Really?" she says with a laugh that pulls at a memory I can't quite place, but it's adorable and makes my chest warm. "That would explain the choice to have more produce for lunch than meat."

"Joker, are you? Well, I can't help that they supposedly have the best garden turkey subs in a hundred mile radius," I dish back.

"Are you a local then?" she asks as she takes another bite. I don't think she's flirting with me, and I can't discern why that seems to bother me a little. Not wanting to be rude and talk with my mouth full, I shake my head. With a sip of Coke, I explain.

"I'm just here to appraise some pieces that a longtime local is considering letting go of. I got into town quite recently, so I'm still fairly new, and this was the best recommendation for a quick lunch," I say.

"So that explains the accent. You travel a lot for work?" she questions deeper as she polishes off half of her hoagie, the savory scent of provolone and freshly sliced Italian deli meats making me regret my salad on a bun.

"Yes, but this is my first time in this part of the states. I've lived just outside of London for all my life. I take it you're not a local either?" I ask. When her brows draw together in confusion and a slight tinge of concern glimmers in her eyes, I recognize how odd that must be without explanation. "I just assumed a local wouldn't be carrying around an entire ream of copy paper and a laptop. Your bag contents look a bit like my own actually."

"Oh, right," she says with a laugh of what I can only assume is relief as she looks over at the tote bag stuffed to the brim with papers. "I'm actually staying here for the summer to finish my research paper for my masters program. My parents are the ones repairing the-"

"-the Corlucius Lighthouse. It's you," I interrupt impulsively to her and to my own surprise. "The couple that hired me mentioned your family."

"It seems like everyone knew I was coming here before I did. I only decided a few days ago, but I guess bad breakups will shake up your plans like that," she shrugs with a swig of her Coca Cola. As soon as the words leave her naturally rosy lips that I can't stop looking at, she flinches at what I'm certain she deems as an overshare. Immediately moving to rectify the supposed awkwardness, she apologizes. "Oh my god, that was a lot. I'm sorry, I just meant I needed a little time away not that I miss him or anything. Not that it matters. Wow, I just keep talking."

"At least you had a relationship," I jest to ease any bit of her discomfort with a truth of my own. "My mother and sister are overbearingly involved in my nonexistent love life now that my sister is married. They're convinced I spend too much of my time working and not enough time pursuing romantic interests. Seems as though reminding them that when the time is right, it'll happen isn't enough."

"That's what my parents believe. When it's meant to happen, you'll know, and the person will seem like an old friend you've spent your whole life knowing," she adds and with a pause, she gathers her wrappers and trash. "At least you're not holding a restraining order."

My eyes widen at the idea that someone out there could cause Dessa to need a restraining order, and I don't like the feeling I have in my chest. I've never been in a physical altercation before, but something tells me if this past flame scared her, I wouldn't hesitate to throw my first punch. I've heard stories from my sister's friends about horrible exes, but it will never cease to amaze me at the lengths small men will go to convince themselves they're owed something. Packing up my belongings and crumbling my sandwich wrapper as well, I look at her, hoping she couldn't see my thoughts written on my face.

"No, I can't say that, but I can say this seems to be a good place to get some air. Living on that island has to feel freeing. I'm over at Morning Glory's. It's a victorian style house they've converted to a cozy bed and breakfast," I offer as we both stand up to toss our trash in the bin. "You should come see it. Shit, I-"

"-Oh," she says at the same moment I swear. I realize I must come across to her that I'm trying to take her home, and I desperately try to correct my words when she surprises me.

"I'm sorry, I didn't mean I was trying to - I mean, I - I don't want to be too forward," I stumble.

"My project is about the history of the keepers, mainly the women that made it all possible, and I'd really appreciate you sharing anything you find that could help me. Even maybe talking to the people you work for? Only if it's not too much trouble," she asks, her hands touching my arm when she worries that she's put me out. Her touch is soothing and delicate, sending a warm comfort through my body like hot chocolate during the first snow of winter.

"Of course, it's no trouble at all. I'd love to help. Maybe we should meet again and share resources. Would you like my phone number? If you're more comfortable with an email address, I can give you that instead. As long as you're comfortable," I add ensuring she doesn't feel pressure in any way. I don't want to become another man in her life that's caused her to feel unsafe. Just the thought again of the man she ran from sends a sharpness through me I don't like.

"Resources," she ponders aloud. "Right, I think you could help actually. Do you have a card?"

I fish a business card from my wallet and place it in her open palm, my fingertips buzzing at the miniscule contact with her skin. The sensation is odd, to feel so familiarly drawn to someone, but I don't mind it at all. Before I know it, my whole hand is aflame with the sensation of her touch as she writes her phone number on my open palm like a pre-teen. It's an adorable juxtaposition to have a brilliant woman doodle on my hand, and I can't hold the silly grin I'm wearing at bay.

When she looks up at me, her green eyes shimmer in the sunlight behind her glasses before she lets go of my hand and I woe the loss instantly. The incessant tug of my memory is desperately trying to place the feeling I have to make logic of it, but the feeling is immune to my attempts to shake it. I feel like I've known her for years. I feel like we haven't only just met. As I'm tossing around the new sensation, she slings her chaotic bag full of papers over her shoulder and puts my card in her back pocket. I tell myself it's so she can keep it safe and not lose it in the Bermuda Triangle of photo copies.

"Thank you for lunch, Theodore. It was nice to meet you," she says sweetly with the softest shade of pink flushing her cheeks again, almost as if she suddenly remembered she's shy.

"Theo," I correct her playfully. "It was a pleasure to meet you too, Odessa."

"Dessa," she returns the bit and we both smile.

Watching her walk out of McNamara's and take a right toward the docks, I think about what I said to my mother and sister about when you get the feeling of someone special. I can't shake the sensation that

I've met Dessa before, or that her smile is what I think the sunshine feels like after a week of rain and clouds back home.

Chapter Nine

Odessa

I don't know what it is about this house, but it makes Dad want to cook enough every night for an entire construction crew. I think he's just really excited to be outside in early summer and not sweat like we did back in the desert. He has the grill on the side of the keeper's house that faces the entrance of the lighthouse so he can keep working on the steps leading up to it. That's the only obstacle left before we're actually able to get to the top of it. We ate dinner at the small picnic table outside that Dad built, and stayed out there talking until the sun started to set.

Carefully stepping between organized piles of paper I copied from the library earlier this morning, I almost trip over the corner of the rug in the middle of the room. I narrowly miss a full disaster, but catch myself on the desk chair, sliding into place in front of my laptop. Looking back at the papers, I let my mind wander to the stories and historical accounts I read about. I've only just clipped the surface of what I know this island and the mainland has to offer when it comes to information. I want my research to feel personal and educational, giving a voice to the lesser known figures that made it all possible, so the best way I work is just to keep reading and let the voices speak through these old photographs, newspaper clippings, and journals.

I jump when I hear Dad clear his throat from the doorway as he makes his way over to the bed to sit down, stepping through my grid of papers on the floor like hopscotch. The part of me that has remained skittish since my encounter with Marcus, makes me angry at him. I hate that he can still affect me even from a distance.

"Hey Kiddo, I didn't mean to scare you. You must be working really hard already. You know you could just take a break for a while before jumping into your project," he offers as his eyes scan the hours of work I've already logged.

"I know, Dad. It just makes me feel better to keep moving on, I think," I say, hoping it'll make sense to him so I don't have to talk about it anymore. I'm instantly relieved when recognition dawns on him. I remember when my Grandma passed away a few years ago, and that was right about the time he bought a new tiny home to renovate and sell instead of taking time off. Maybe I inherited this type of trauma response from him.

"Looks like you got a good start. Are you heading back into town tomorrow then?" he asks, picking up the piece of paper closest to his foot and looking it over casually.

"Yeah, I umm, I met a few people who are going to help me dig up more, so I might meet up with him-them," I say without being able to hide the word and I see my dad's brow twitch. "I just mean the ladies from the library and, well, I met someone named Theo who's working with some locals to appraise their antiques and some things they've found in their houses and stuff. Don't worry, I won't jump into anything."

"Hey hey your mother and I aren't judging," he chuckles. "Speaking of Mom, if you're by the store, can you pick her up some cold medicine? She's coming down with something. It just seemed to kick her ass out of nowhere too, so she's convinced she needs to quarantine herself for a day or so to make sure it doesn't throw us off the progress of the reno. Can't have us both out of commission." He shrugs.

"Yeah, I'll grab some stuff while I'm out. Just have her text me what she wants me to get if she feels up to it. Otherwise, I'll just get her what she always gets me."

"A day off school to watch The Price is Right while you eat an entire box of popsicles?" Dad laughs, running his hands through his salt and pepper hair like he could touch the memory in his mind if he wanted to.

"Say what you want, but that was a magical remedy for everything. Still is," I say with a smirk, jumping into that warm pool of nostalgia with him. I swear I can still taste the artificial cherry flavor of my favorite popsicle, and remember all of the ridiculously cheesy jokes printed on the sticks.

"Well, while she's in there trying to get that fever down, I'm hoping I can surprise her with finished steps. I promised her a dinner for two at the top of that lighthouse when we can make it up there, so I better get my ass in gear," he mentions. I know he's presenting it to me as her her expectation of him, but he can't hide the soft glint in his eyes at the thought of it. For as long as I can remember, my parents have been in love. For as long as they've been together, their roles may have shifted from being spouses to parents, but the one thing that's remained a constant is their love of dating each other.

"Then you better Youtube how to make something other than burgers on that grill," I joke and he holds a hand over his heart in an exaggerated motion, as if to hold in the blood from the mortal wound I just delivered over his ability to burn a burger.

"Ouch kiddo, my heart," he chuckles and stands up to walk to my door, avoiding the papers again on the way out. Kicking the corner of the rug that always seems to flip on purpose, his step causes a loud creak to cry from the wood beneath him. "Remind me to look at that floorboard," he mutters on the way out the door and down the hallway.

Turning back to my laptop, I reread the notes I added to my findings from tonight's research. I don't even realize almost two hours have passed, when my phone loudly vibrates on the edge of my desk. The sound of it against the old wood of the desk is an odd juxtaposition that transports me to another place where I'm just a girl sitting near her window in the 1700's watching the clouds slowly drift over the moon. It's the reason I fell in love with learning history - the idea that time can overlap in a single place, where I can exist somewhere that countless others over centuries of time have existed. Sometimes it's overwhelming to try to process, but the more I learn, the more the vision becomes clearer. When I was a kid, it was just a thought. In high school, it was like a detailed flipbook. Now, it's like I'm watching a movie in my mind where it starts in black and white and morphs into color with details I never knew to see before my masters program. I can't wait for what I'll see after I finish my doctorate.

As I reach for my phone, it gives two distinctly different vibrations. Swiping up to clear the lock screen, I crease my brows at the first notification.

Unknown Caller ID

There's no number. Just a missed call and no voicemail. My gut settles and I do my best to ignore the tiny seedling of anxiety that takes root in my solar plexus. *No*, I tell myself, *he's not here and he doesn't know where I am or how to find me. He can't reach me. I'm safe here.*

Shaking myself out of the pit I almost slipped into, I notice the other notification is a text. Smiling at the thought of Aly and Savannah sending me nightly photos of what they're calling "Mildred's Summer Retreat" has made this experience even more relaxing. But when I open my messages, I realize it's not from Mildred's vacation home.

Theo: Did you make it back to the island alright or did you stop to steal someone else's meal along the way, Dessa?

I can hear his voice in my mind as I read it, and not even the apocalypse could stop the way my body reacts to how I imagine him saying my name. When we'd exchanged numbers at McNamara's after lunch, I just assumed he'd take the standard three days to contact me again. I even recounted our entire interaction in a series of voice memos to Aly and Savannah on the ferry ride back to Corlucius Island to make absolutely certain the possible chemistry was definitely there. As soon as I read his text for the fourth time, I send a screenshot to Aly.

Me: We just met and you already know me so well. That little old lady didn't stand a chance haha

Theo: I'll have to be more diligent with safeguarding my lunch tomorrow then.

Me: Lunch?

Theo: Yes, the meal that's between breakfast and dinner. Do Americans not have lunch?

Me: I was trying to scroll back to the part where you asked me to have lunch with you. In America we ask each other out on a date before assuming. Do they not do that in England?

Theo: You want me to ask you out on a date then, yes?

He catches my words before I do, and although I'm a little on the mortified side for seeming so presumptuous, he doesn't make me simmer in it too long before following up with another text.

Theo: Alright, Dessa. It's a yes. A date tomorrow then.

Me: Wait, I asked you out on a date?

Theo: You definitely did. You're very convincing. How could I decline?

Me: Fine, just don't be late. Noon at the library.

As I stare at the little bubbles at the bottom of the screen, I become suddenly aware of how ridiculous I must look with the size of the smile

I'm wearing. I screenshot the last part of the conversation to Aly to help keep me in check so my expectations aren't unreasonable. I tend to see what I want to see, and it leads to unrealistic hopes at times. I can't help it. I love love - especially when it's new and sometimes it can make my rose colored glasses pretty foggy. How can I not though when I'm surrounded by perfect love and I see it in the way love was capsulated in history.

> Aly: Sweetie he's def interested lol you have to tell us what happens tomorrow

> Aly: Sav says don't wear leggings

Before I can respond with a sarcastic comment, my phone rings once and hangs up with another call from an Unknown ID. I can't fight the unease that slowly covers me like molasses. I know unknown numbers are mostly spam, and that's probably what this is, but it still makes me uncomfortable. I put my phone on the small nightstand's charger and close my laptop, intent on getting a good night's sleep for another day of research on the mainland.

I pull the desk lamp's chain to turn it off, and the moment the room darkens, the outside becomes clearer. I can see the edge of the island where the jagged rocks meet the sea, and the reflection of the moonlight on the water is like a painting. What catches my eye is the shadowed figure walking among the rocks, and I rub my hands quickly over the window's glass like the night before to clear the illusion, but when I do, the figure doesn't go away. It pauses to look up at me and a chill rakes through my body like I've never felt. It's so fast I don't even realize I'm screaming until my dad is racing into the room and over to me, my papers on the floor flying and the creak of the floorboard echoing.

He pulls me to him protectively and all I can do is point at the window. Turning the lights on, he squints to see what I'm pointing at that could have caused my reaction. I drag myself out of panic to verbalize my fear.

"He's out t-there, Dad," I manage to say through hyperventilation-induced breaths and furious heart beats I can feel down to my toes. "M-Marcus."

Looking back and forth and cupping his hands on the window to either side of his face, he stares intently for minutes silently, as if he could hear a footstep through the glass. When he comes back to me, his eye contact tells me what I know he's going to say. My heart rate drops, and the exhaustion kicks in as he pulls me into a hug.

"There's no one there, kiddo. You're ok," he says confidently and reassuringly. "It's just a shadow from the moonlight. He can't get to you here. You're safe."

Swaying me back and forth with a hand on my head, I know he's right. When I open my eyes to glance back out into the darkness, I see the same spot empty.

There's no one there.

CHAPTER TEN

THEODORE

*T*he storm. Being surrounded by darkness this powerful is akin to being swallowed by a whale. At the mercy of it, I hold onto the only thing I can reach, the edge of the ship. With both hands I accept that I am nothing in the face of this monster as I weather the swell of the waves against the beating of the wind. There are faint cries amidst the claps of thunder, screams of anguish and pain, but they are as lost as we are in the tempest. Amidst their cries dances a haunting hymn, a song I can't hear anywhere but my own mind. I look into the distance, for what, I'm not sure, but with the whip of the wind, my body is thrashed and thrown somewhere even darker. I float, I gasp, I struggle. The light never comes - the light I know will lead me home to the heavenly paradise I was promised. The song curls around my heart, giving warmth to the limbs I know can't keep me on this mortal plane much longer. Thunder and lightning compel the waves to rage, but I am at peace with my promise. My promise I can never forget.

The clap of thunder as loud as a cannon shakes me awake in my now sweat-soaked sheets and wallpapered room. It takes me a few minutes to catch my bearings and remember exactly where I am. I look over at the window when something odd catches my attention. Walking over to it in my boxers, I can't explain what I see. The night is calm and clear, the moon is bright, and everything is still. There is no storm to be seen and there is no sign of the cause of thunder that shook me awake.

Running a hand through my dark hair, I take a few swigs from the bottled water I left on the nightstand, and sit on the edge of the bed to remind myself of my surroundings. The digital alarm clock reads 3:13am. I haven't had nightmares like that since I was a youngster, and I can only blame the change in environment and the beam from the old lighthouse for pulling me back into it. It seemed so real that I'd be willing to swear that the floral sheets of this bed and breakfast weren't drenched in sweat, but sea water. Shaking my head, I pull the flat sheet from the bed and lay it over the chair in the corner and trade it for the thin knitted afghan on its seat.

Flipping the pillow to the cold side, I settle back into bed, my body feeling the seductive pull of a deep sleep. As my eyes close, a song plays through my mind and lulls me into the darkness.

***

Mrs. Sarah Goodman tops off my glass of freshly squeezed lemonade while her husband, George, fetches the next box from the storage stockpile in the garage. They've consolidated a lot of their belongings over the past few months, and with the amount of space they'll need for their son to move back home after a failed marriage, they are hoping to sell what they can. The local maritime museum has reached out to them, and Sarah agreed to donate what she and George don't want to sell.

While they're both in their late 70's, George has taken up pickleball and is surprisingly limber carrying boxes to the living room. Sarah, on the other hand, has made no mention of a desire to participate in league sports. She does, however, have a very healthy bookshelf of bodice rippers as my mum calls them. Judging by the severity of cracked book spines, I wager her imagination is even more active than George's pickleball game.

"Tell George what you just told me, dear," Sarah says with the look of joy only true gossip can bring - I would know, my sister wears it often. She pulls him by the leg of his trousers until he comes to sit next to her on the couch. Placing a small shoebox of items on the coffee table between us, George takes a sip of his lemonade and laces his fingers with hers. The small gesture is a bit warming considering my mum and dad split when I was in primary school.

"I was just telling Mrs. Goodman here-"

"-Sarah!" she interjects to correct me for the second time. George smiles wider as she nods for me to continue after her interruption.

"I was just telling Sarah that I had lunch at McNamara's yesterday and you were right. It was the best sandwich I've had in a long time," I admit. It's not even a lie to appease them for the recommendation, it's genuinely true. I may be just a little biased due to the unexpected company, but still, it can only help.

"Charlene rang me last night and said you were dining with quite the looker. Her husband is the one you must have ordered your subs with," Sarah says with a sly smile. *Sly, indeed.*

"Oh yes," I answer and try to keep her imagination from spiraling into the pages of one of her Fabio-covered novels on the shelf. "Seems we're both new in town for work. That was Odessa. Her parents bought the Corlucius Island property."

"Oh that's David and Becca's girl! That's right. Poor darling, Charlene says she's staying with her parents this summer so her old boyfriend will leave her be. I'm glad you two met, then. You can explore this place together, you know. It's always nice to have a friend," Sarah explains, more to herself in rambling as George separates their hands to open the old shoebox on the table.

"Well, that's good. It sounds like a nice way to spend your spare time here," George remarks. Sarah sighs a little, most likely disappointed he didn't fully indulge in her gossip and excitement over the attempt to possibly matchmake Dessa and I. I don't actually mind the thought of that last bit. "Take her to The Broken Mast for a nicer meal, son."

As the phone rings, George excuses himself and I eye the contents of the box. Pulling out a handkerchief, I open it to find a brass pocket watch stopped at precisely 3:13am, and the image of the red numbers on my digital alarm clock stand out in my mind. My brows crease at the oddity, but I don't have time to dwell on it before Sarah places her hand on my wrist, drawing me out from under the train of thought before it runs me over.

"Has Odessa happened to mention anything about the lighthouse?" she whispers and I can't quite place her intentions, or what she's hoping for in my response. When she sees my confusion, she looks to the kitchen where George answered the phone to make sure he's out of earshot before she continues. "People say it's haunted, you know. All kinds of things happened there."

When I instinctively chuckle, I notice the slight tinge of offense she takes at my reaction. Of course, I don't mean any offense at all, but she can't be serious, can she? When I return the eye contact, I realize she is indeed absolutely serious. To avoid any interruption of the business relationship we've entered, I immediately bounce back.

"Is it? I hadn't heard," I say, the expression in her eyes relaxing as she leans in to tell me more.

"Not a believer, hmm?" she decides. "Careful, dear. Lots of us take it very seriously. The past runs deep through these generations, and ghosts are nothing but walking pages of a history book you've never read. Nothing good has ever come from staying at the keeper's house. Always ends in death one way or another. Many have tried, but when it went up for sale after the last owners passed suddenly, we were glad to see it go to those people. We thought maybe the renovations will bring it back to its former glory and the ghosts will be able to rest after all this time."

"Do people...see ghosts often there?" I ask carefully, trying to get more information without seeming too indulgent in the fantastical, although I can't say I'm not a believer.

"They know they're there. It's the lights, the smells, the sounds, things moving so they're not where you left them. I'd say it's the usual stuff, but not for doubters," Sarah teases.

"It's not that I don't believe. I've just never been face-to-face with a reason why I should. I mean no disrespect to you or to the history here."

"Maybe it's a blessing you haven't seen them," she shrugs and sips her lemonade as George hangs up the phone. On his way back into the living room, she leans in to add one more thing. "Doesn't mean they can't see *you*."

***

Well on my way to The Broken Mast upon George's recommendation, I replay the whispered conversation - or was it a warning? - from Sarah. I've never been a superstitious man, but Mum is and she's dragged my younger sister into it as well. The psychics, the ghost stories, the hopes of what lies beyond are always threatening to surface when we talk, but I've never felt the pull of it like they do. Doesn't mean it's not there, I suppose.

I snap myself out of it when another text from Dessa comes through.

> Dessa: You're late, Theo. I'm deducting five points from Ravenclaw.

> Me: How do you know I've been sorted to Ravenclaw? And I still have 45 seconds before I'm late.

Just as I turn the corner, I spot her for a brief second before she sees me, and it's an image I'm desperately trying to burn into my memory. Her long brunette curls dance around her in the breeze like she's underwater, and her glasses frame her eyes as they reflect the smile radiating from her pink lips. She's holding her phone like it's precious, and I realize in that same moment, it's my response that's got her in a blush. When she sees me approaching, she taps her watch and I speed my steps to make it to her with three seconds to spare.

Looking up at me as I playfully smirk down at her, I fight the urge to cradle her into my arms like a long distance lover's reunion. Her long satin dress with a denim oversized jacket seems to tell me she's dressed up, but not too much, and her makeup is subtle, but present.

She couldn't be anymore darling, and I don't know how I'm going to resist the siren's call of her lips for another day.

"Come on, let's get you some lunch before you inhale someone else's," I say with a smirk and she returns it, letting me place my hand on the small of her back on the way inside. The feel of her beneath my palm sends a fluttering wave through my body unexpectedly. It's a strange sensation, but I can't deny that it feels strangely...*right*.

CHAPTER ELEVEN

ODESSA

Following the hostess to our table, we were seated in what has to be known as the best seat in the house. It's in the back near the window that faces the open ocean, and there isn't a single word that could sum up its beauty. As we slide into our booth seats across from each other, I feel underdressed for whatever this occasion is. We may have playfully called this a date over text, but it's one thing to be bold behind a screen and completely another to look into the eyes of someone that oddly makes you want to kick your feet and twirl your hair.

He catches me looking at him one second too long and he smiles. Like the giddy idiot I'm apparently morphing into, I smile back - wider than I intend to as I curse myself internally for not only showing my cards, but throwing them at him. When our server comes by to say hello and deliver ice waters with a slice of lemon, he smiles sweetly at us before handing us the small one page menu. *Jesus, I might as well write "Everyone look at me! I have big crush on this sexy Brit!" on my forehead. Wait, I have a crush? Oh my god, I think I do. How old am I?*

"Do you want to try the oysters or the fried lobster ravioli for an appetizer?"

"Hmm? Oh, umm, yes. Thank you," I awkwardly stumble, and we both laugh when I realize how I answered the simplest of questions.

"Good idea," he says to me, not letting me marinate in my mental self deprecation. Turning to our server, Lance, according to his gold engraved nametag, Theo continues. "You heard her, we'll do both the oysters and fried lobster ravioli to start."

Lance nods with a grin, and walks away with a sway to his step no doubt mentally calculating the 20% gratuity already. I look back to Theo, who is looking at me like he's trying to remember me, and it's the weirdest sensation because it's how I've been looking at him too. With a tilt of his head, I open the conversation as I sip my water to give my lips something else to do besides imagine how his feel.

"How's your work going? You mentioned you're in contact with a local family?" I ask with genuine curiosity as I pick up a warm roll of bread from the basket in the center of the table.

"Interesting actually, it's Sarah and George Goodman. Their families have apparently lived here for so many generations, there aren't records of them anywhere else. It's quite remarkable really. They're trying to move out some of their storage, so they hired me to aid them in appraising their collection to see what they'll sell and what they'll eventually donate to the Historical Society and the Maritime Museum downtown," he explains, and I can't help but lean forward, my mind racing with what could be in their home.

"That sounds incredible. To be able to hold something in your hands that has been held by someone else so long ago. It's what got me into history. I like to feel the connection to the past no matter how much the world advances, you know?" I say. When I snap out of my ramble, I realize that instead of being bored or staring at his phone like

Marcus used to, Theo is completely locked into my every word. "Sorry, sometimes I get lost in how much I love it."

"Don't ever apologize for being interested in something, especially something as fascinating as history. Not a lot of people find it as appealing as we do, I'm afraid. It makes you even more...unique," he says, but in a way that makes me feel like he can see me naked through my clothes, and I'm not shy for once.

"It's nice to be able to fangirl over something and someone else fan...boys over it too?" I smile, and he laughs. It's the kind of laugh that melts butter. It's warm and genuine, making me feel like we've been here a thousand times. There's an odd sense of comfortability in this place, with him.

"I fanboyed over a brass pocket watch today," Theo says as our appetizers arrive balanced on Lance's inner arms. "How's your project coming along?"

As we look over the two plates, we decide to order our entrees while we continue to bask in the ease of conversation and companionship. The table is only silent for a minute before we're both groaning in delight at the level of deliciousness The Broken Mast has to offer. At this point, I don't even need to try another foodie spot. I would gladly survive the entire summer choosing one thing from this menu every day. It takes me a moment to swallow the mouthful of ravioli before I can finally answer him.

"It's going to be a process, but I'm really thankful to be doing the work here in person regardless of my circumstances. My parents gave me a list of people to interview, but I started out in the library first so I can get some of the foundation work done. I don't want to retell what you can read in a textbook, but as I'm sure you know, history is written about men by men, and I want to highlight the invisible labor of the women who fueled so much of the trade and success of this part of the world," I say with all my heart, quickly realizing the soapbox he must think I've jumped onto.

"That's a well-needed approach for most of world history, isn't it?" Theo adds and I pause mid-bite of my fifth oversized ravioli. He smiles and creases his brow. "You expected a different response?"

"No, I just - well, ok, maybe?" I answer honestly, the flashbacks of talking to Marcus about anything of historical importance, especially the countless uncelebrated contributions of women, and his exaggerated sigh audible in my mind.

"A little about me, if it's not too much to share on our first date," he starts, and pauses to indulge in the way the wording causes me to hold in a smile. I cram the first bite of my entree that's now in front of me into my mouth so my lips can do something other than curl at the corners everytime he looks at me like that. "A little about me is that my sister and I were raised only by my mother. She is easily the hardest working woman I've ever met. When Dad left, she didn't want us to feel the loss or the heartache, so she worked two jobs and picked up handling people's alterations. We never wanted for anything. We didn't know until high school that Dad was never even sending us birthday and holiday cards with gift money, it was her."

"She sounds so strong," I add out loud without realizing it, a mouthful of lump crab cake in my cheeks. Swallowing, I correct the unintentional lack of table manners. "Sorry."

"It's alright. She is. When Greta and I realized what she was doing for us, we both got part time jobs after school, and it allowed her to reclaim some of the life she'd so easily sacrificed for us," he finishes. "Your project will undoubtedly uncover the other women that also sacrificed and put everyone else first like she did. I think it's not only admirable, but necessary. It's really beautiful, Dessa."

I let his words sink in while we both enjoy the meal, the crisp lemon water, and the fact that we can connect on something so deeply important at the same time. A few minutes go by and Lance swings through to clear the empty appetizer plates, glad to hear that we're still enjoying our experience.

"I'm still sorry you had to go through that, and I'm sorry she did too. I'm grateful every single second for being lucky enough to have my parents. Sometimes it's hard to feel like I deserve it, especially after everything with Marcus," I admit softly as I stare out the window at the afternoon sun on the sea. I'm lost in it momentarily until I feel Theo's hand on top of mine, his warmth sending a rush through my entire body from that single comforting touch.

"I don't know your ex, but I promise you it's not your fault, and your parents do not blame you at all for this. You couldn't have possibly known. People like him hide who they are. They're darkness," he says, and I make eye contact with him as he helps me grant myself the permission to admit that what happened wasn't something I could have predicted.

"Darkness is an interesting choice of words, but honestly it's really fitting now that I think about it," I realize.

"Ah, yet another contribution from my mum. She always told Greta and I that there are mostly two types of people on Earth. There are people that seek out light to lead them to whatever it is they're looking for. Perhaps they're sad, or unhappy, or lost in the world."

"What's the other type?" I ask curiously, my belly full and my attention held captive. He has yet to remove his hand from mine and I hope he doesn't. I use my other hand to rest under my jaw, holding my head up as I listen to his stories.

"They're the lights - the people that can't help but shine," he says almost with a dreamy look, and I wish with all my heart someone like him would look at me like that. *Ok, I wish with all my heart Theo would look at me like that.*

"Which one are you, Theo?" I wonder quietly, but it comes out a little breathier than I plan, and I can't help but notice the slight change in his expression. It's a change that seems intrigued.

"I've always searched for what I don't know exists," he answers cryptically without breaking eye contact, and I feel his soft tone like feathers on my skin.

"And...me?" I ask, not sure myself, but hoping to keep us in this small bubble where time stands still, and I can't stand at all because my knees are weak. He chuckles and my heart splashes into a pool of embarrassment. *I shouldn't be allowed to speak.*

"How can you not see that you're a light?" Theo answers and squeezes my hand. My heart rises and my soul sings to a melody I've never heard, but that I just know. We're frozen, staring at each other in our small corner booth, and I don't know what to say that won't sound ridiculous.

"My best friends said that my ex tried to dim my light," I add, not knowing why. And Theo shakes his head.

"Only a weak man extinguishes a flame he knows he can't fuel. The best thing you can do is what Greta taught herself in high school when she was being bullied - no matter what, shine so bright, they burn."

"I think your sister is my long lost best friend," I smile and he laughs, a sound I don't think I'll ever get bored of even though we've only just met. It feels like I've missed it.

"She'd say the same for you, I'm sure of it. Actually, if you wanted to speak to Sarah Goodman, I'm certain she'd enjoy that - as long as you're open to hearing her fantastical ghost stories about your new family home over there."

I know he's laughing it off, but something uneasy settles around me. I offer a similar chuckle, but I know the moment I'm able to talk to her, I'm going to find out exactly what she knows about the lighthouse. I know most historical places have stories of mystery that surround them, but having been a little creeped out already, I can't fight the curiosity to know more.

Finishing our lunch and walking to the dock with our fingers brushing gently together every few steps, I dread boarding the small boat that will take me away from him. It was only lunch, I know, but it felt like it flew by. When we reach the dock, and I see the boat fired up to depart, I turn to say goodbye to Theo, but my body is thrown into shock when he pulls me into him.

Without a word, the bond between us is yanked tightly, and he tucks my unruly wind-swept waves behind my ear. Every cell in my body vibrates in anticipation, and they celebrate in perfect unison when his hand remains on my jaw, tilting my head up to allow our lips to meet gently at first. At the first chance when my mouth opens slightly, his tongue slides in and I will myself not to moan right into his tonsils. The shake of the world around us breaks the moment, pulling us apart, as we share a look of confusion.

"You felt that right?" I ask concerned and he nods curiously. It was if a soft shockwave rippled through and past us, but no one else walking by reacted. Just as I open my mouth to speak, the captain of the small boat yells over to me that visiting time is over, and we'll be back tomorrow. With a soft kiss to the top of my head, Theo releases me from his hold and I mourn the loss instantly. He reassures he'll text me before I load myself and my shopping bag onto the boat.

***

Returning to the island, I look at the approaching lighthouse through different eyes. I imagine the countless others that have sailed the same sea looking for the same light. As I notice a movement up at the lantern room at the top, I can see the dark figure of a man, my dad, pacing. I'm excited the closer we get, almost anxious, that he's finished the stairs so we can finally see what lies inside it.

As I say goodnight to the ferryman, I look up to the lighthouse once more time and see the figure of my father walk into the lantern room. I try yelling up to him, but he must be too busy to hear me. Looking down at my laptop bag and the two small bags I grabbed from the drugstore for Mom, I walk up to the keeper's house, and what I see stops me dead in my tracks.

There's my father, walking out of the keeper's house, he nods and takes a gulp of his beer. I've never really seen my dad drink that much, so it's still a bit weird to see him walking around the house in the middle of the afternoon with an open can.

"Hey Dad, did you find anything cool up there?" I ask and point. His expression remains clueless.

"I haven't been up there yet, but when I do, you'll know it," he offers casually with a small hint of underlying irritation, and I remind myself not to push my dad when he's tired. "I've just been working on small shit around this place so I could stay close to your mom. She's still feeling a little off, so thanks for picking up her cough syrup. She's excited to spend time with you, so just stop in and say hi to her, kiddo."

Dad pats my back and I head inside, unable to shake the impossible image of a man pacing back and forth at the top of the Corlucius Lighthouse.

CHAPTER TWELVE

ODESSA

I gently knock on my parent's bedroom door, and I instantly feel like a kid telling their mom about a bad dream. When I don't hear anything from the other side of the door, I push it open slowly and step inside with a bag full of get well soon necessities. Catching the first glimpse of my mom, I wonder if I bought enough. She's laying in bed, bundled up with a light sheen of sweat covering her brow. Tossing and turning, she's wide awake when what sounds like a rib-cracking coughing fit seizes her.

Rushing over to her, I hand her the small glass of water she points to on the nightstand, and I sit with her as she takes small sips to ease her cough. When it finally subsides, she sighs in exhausted annoyance and sits up a little farther against the headboard. As strong as my mom is, it's so difficult to see her look so tired and frail. I know it's a cold, but damn, she looks like she's fighting off something a lot tougher.

"I brought you some stuff from town," I offer, moving to sit next to her before she puts a hand out to stop me.

"Honey, I don't want to get you sick," she says, holding a hand out to take the paper bag of assorted items I grabbed from the pharmacy.

I put the handles to rest on her open palm, but when I let go, it's like the bag suddenly weighs ninety pounds as it plops onto her comforter. "This was so sweet of you. Thank you."

"Dad wasn't very specific with what you needed, so I picked what I thought you'd like. I figured I'd grab a bunch and you'd have options," I respond with a shrug. Mom laughs softly in a controlled effort not to reintroduce another coughing fit. When I look at her curiously, she shakes her head.

"Dad tries, but I'm glad you're here to help him out. He's not great at the domestic stuff and I think it frustrates him," she explains. "I think having you here makes him feel a little better. When I had covid years ago he shrank a whole load of laundry, and I got to him just in time before he put dish soap in the dishwasher."

That makes me laugh out loud. The idea that my brilliant contractor of a father pulling my mom's shirts out of the dryer only to realize they would be a better fit for an American Girl doll than Mom is hilarious.

"Oh my god, were you pissed?" I ask through a laugh. She shakes her head as she digs through the bag.

"Actually, he was pissed at himself. After that, he lived on a media diet of tutorials and vowed to never be outsmarted by an appliance ever again. I didn't have to do laundry or dishes for so long afterward just because he wanted to prove to himself he wasn't a useless man in the house he helped to build," she says. "I know he needs us though."

Mom lays the contents of the now empty bag on the bed, and now that I look at it, you'd think I was a school nurse at a scout camp. There's cough syrup for night and day, cough drops in three flavors, ginger ale, orange juice, a tabloid magazine I didn't even know was still in print, Pepto Bismol, Tylenol, Advil, crackers, soup, a candy bar, tissues, and a dinosaur pez dispenser. As she looks at the plastic green dinosaur she tilts her head as I reach for it.

"Ok, that was for me," I chuckle. Putting it in my purse, she takes another sip of water and opens the cough syrup, curling her nose at the artificial cherry flavor I can smell from where I'm standing. "Just rest up, and I'll work with Dad so there's no missed content, ok? Is there anything else you need?"

"Oh, speaking of Dad, could you just find a nice way to tell him to smoke his cigars outside? That tobacco smell has been turning my stomach," she asks before taking the meds with a grimace, and then sliding back down to curl up in the blankets.

"You got it. I'll be nice and not throw them in the ocean even though they're gross," I say with a smile knowing my mom completely agrees. I blow her a kiss which she returns with a smile and closes her eyes.

Slipping out of the room, I head down the small wooden staircase to relay the message to Dad who I can still hear working on the lighthouse steps. Not bothering to slip on my shoes, I walk through the grass mindful of every step, and loving the way the summer sun warms each blade it touches. As I approach Dad, he's drinking what looks to be his fourth beer which I surmise by the pile of cans that's catching the low rays of light between the clouds. He's working hard on hammering away, but his movements look ever so slightly slowed. When I reach his side, he slides his safety glasses up and kisses my head.

"Hey kiddo, you give your mother the stuff from the pharmacy?" he asks as he leans against the side of the lighthouse that used to be all white before time stripped it away in pieces. I nod and he puts a hand on my shoulder in thanks.

"She's not looking so good, you know," I remind him. "I hope it helps her, oh, and she wants you to please keep your cigars outside and not smoke them in the house, Dad. You really should just quit. They're not good for you."

"What are you talking about?" he asks with a look that can only be described as confusion with a drop of offense for taste.

"The smoke. She said it's turning her stomach and it's probably not helping her cough, you know?" I explain, hoping the message is clear enough that I don't have to keep going. I hate the feeling of being in the middle of them, but this issue has been bothering me ever since he picked up the habit a few years ago.

"I haven't smoked one since we've been here," he says as his expression twists further into confusion.

"Dad, it's ok if you do, she just wants it to be outside, ok?" I add carefully and without any judgement. I have no right to be judgemental as a 30-something masters student living free with my parents after a disastrous breakup, but I cringe a little at the fact he's hiding it.

"Kiddo, I haven't. It's just been a couple beers here and there. No cigars because I don't want to try to get that smell out of a house I'm going to sell. It's a no brainer, so relax. I promise I haven't," he reassures me and his tone is so sincere, there's no way he's lying. And he wouldn't lie. Maybe the smell has been lingering from a past owner.

"Well, why don't I make us something to absorb your liquid lunch?" I say playfully as he rolls his eyes, giving in to the casual family bond we've always had with each other. They were a little more strict while I was in school, but ever since college, it's like they turned into my wise friends and not my strict parents. "Maybe a little more chicken parm and a little less burny burger tonight?"

"Your loss," he answers with a shove to my shoulder. "You know you love your Dad's grill master skills."

"You keep telling yourself that, old man," I say back as we both share a grin while the sun sets a little lower on the horizon.

I turn to walk back to the house, trying to take mental stock of what's actually in the pantry after I made myself suddenly hungry for the chicken parm recipe Savannah shared with me. At the halfway point between the lighthouse and the keeper's house, I'm stopped by the surreal beauty of my surroundings and how lucky I am to have the chance to be exactly where I am with the people I love doing what I love to do. With a deep breath to remember this moment, I suddenly still with the prickling sensation of being watched. Swinging my head back the way I came, I see my dad back at work on the steps, and I crease my brows in panic at the feeling rushing its way through my veins.

A slight movement catches my eye, and I twist my head toward the edge of the island where the jagged rocks meet the sea. No need to squint my eyes this time. The blurry shadowed figure I've seen from my window is now standing on the end of the dock, steps away from the soft grass, and close enough that I can't deny what I'm seeing. A man. A man that shouldn't be here. *It's supposed to be safe here.* Cursing myself for not wearing my glasses for once, I don't give myself time to squint to meet his gaze before the sharp, cold fingers of fear lock around my throat, threatening to suffocate me. Fighting the freeze, I pull a shallow breath into my lungs and release a scream as I turn to run, but everything moves in slow motion like a dream.

I blink twice before realizing that the grip on my body I thought was fear is my dad, shaking me with both hands until I rejoin the world of the conscious. Desperately trying to catch my breath, I stop screaming as he looks me over with concern.

"What is it?" he asks, his tone laced with worry. His brows draw together as his eyes conduct a scan to evaluate my status. My eyes dart behind his head to the rocky edge where the man was watching me, but as it was before, there's no one there. It's empty.

"I saw-there was-I..." I stutter as my body loses its fight or flight rigidity, and I release the tension in my shoulders. I know Dad can feel the shift as he lets go, patting my shoulder while I continue trying to make sense of what's happening. "I keep seeing a man standing over there, Dad. It's scaring the shit out of me."

"There's nothing there, Kiddo, I promise. He can't get to you here. No one can. I made sure of it," he reassures me as he looks over his shoulder to where I had concentrated my gaze sans glasses. When he turns back to me, his slightly bloodshot eyes soften. For a brief moment, I have a distinct parallel memory where he's checking my closet for monsters to convince me it was just a dream.

"I'm sorry," I mumble, frustrated at the feeling of embarrassment that's quickly flooding my veins like embalming fluid. Shaking my head in disappointment toward myself, I unlock the door in my mind to let reason and rationality back inside. "I know you're right, I just keep seeing him."

"You need to be getting more sleep," Dad suggests. "I can hear you at night, Dess. It hurts us to hear you so upset." He pulls me into a hug, his hand resting on the back of my wavy chestnut hair, instantly transporting me to the safety of my childhood.

"Hear what?" I ask, pulling away as I process his words. He looks at me with a softness in his sympathetic expression, and I can see his worry, but I don't know what he's talking about.

"I can hear you in your room crying every night. You don't have to hide it, Kiddo. I know you're taking this breakup hard especially after what happened, but I want you to remember I won't let anyone near you out here," he says with conviction. Cradling my cheeks in his palms, he continues with a determination in his eyes. "I'm your father, and I'll always keep you safe. I'll never let him come here to take you away, you understand me?"

I nod to acknowledge his protectiveness and sense of paternal duty, but I can't shake the oddity of his actions and choice of words. My agreement seems to ease his concern as he pulls me back into the embrace that reminds me of my post night terror Mom and Dad hug sandwich remedy. It's not that I'm not used to being comforted by my dad, but something is nagging at the back of my mind as he rocks me in his hold with the sound of the sea to calm my nerves.

Why does he think I've been crying every night?

CHAPTER THIRTEEN

ODESSA

I knock on my parents' bedroom door twice with my foot, my hands full with the two bowls of chicken noodle soup I bought in town. Almost too warm for my hands, I remind myself it's mind over body as I push the door open to find the nearest surface to put them down. Walking into the room, Mom pushes herself up in the bed, propping her back against the pillows and wooden headboard.

Offering her a soft smile, I place both bowls on her nightstand amongst the cough syrup bottles, coffee mug, and bag of cough drops I bought for her. She hasn't improved, but from what we can all tell, it's not something highly contagious as Dad and I have been taking turns checking on her, and sneaking in for meals and quality time. With her wheat-colored hair wrapped up in a messy bun, she offers me a grin in return - a grin that widens when she sees that I plan on having lunch with her.

Without a word, Mom slides over in the bed to make room for me and I join her. As we blow ripples across the surface of our soup in tandem, she nudges her shoulder to mine.

"Thanks for taking care of me, sweetheart. I can't imagine going through this...whatever it is...without you and your dad," she says before sipping the first spoonful of broth. I can tell it soothes her when she closes her eyes as the warmth travels from her throat to her chest. Sighing, she opens her eyes and in them shines the love she feels even now through her cold.

"We can't help it. We love you, you know," I answer playfully, joining her in sipping my broth. "Anything you need. Hey, maybe we should get you a little bell or something like in the movies."

"I wouldn't even have to ring it with how attentive your father is being. I keep reminding him he doesn't need to stay in here with me every night, but he's so stubborn. You know how he gets, but it's like I'm a kid again. Petting my hair and even singing me to sleep, he must be anxious for me to get back to work," she says sweetly with a soft smile. Seeing my dad as the strong man he is, I always love the way he dotes on her. He can be as tough as he wants, but Mom and I are the kryptonite.

"Maybe you should fake it for a while, Mom. That sounds pretty nice," I jest, and she laughs in return with a wink.

"You know, I thought about that too," she admits as we giggle into our chicken noodle soup bowls that have stopped steaming. In unison, as if we were marionettes attached to the same strings, we sip the first few spoonfuls cautiously before diving in. "How has your research been going? Meet anyone in town to help you?"

"I've made some friends in the library, and I had lunch at McNamara's and The Broken Mast and-"

"-you ate at The Broken Mast alone?" Mom asks, and before I realize what I've revealed, she narrows her eyes like she's discovered a steaming cup of tea. One thing about Mom and I? We love to gossip, and right now, she's looking at me knowing I just accidentally served the hottest cup. I can't help but match her growing grin when she knows I have a secret.

"Noooo," I say tauntingly with a slurp of soup.

"Rule of the house," she declares matter-of-factly with her spoon pointed upwards to make her point. "No secrets on Corlucius Island. Didn't you watch that episode on the plane? Are they cute? Did they pay? Spill. It."

"Why do I feel like this is going to break into a song from Grease again?" I laugh remembering the days in middle school we'd all dance around the kitchen singing when I admitted to liking my first crush.

"Tell me more! Tell me more!" Mom sings, the last word breaking off a little while she drinks some water to quell the surfacing cough. To keep her voice intact, and not work her up too much, I roll my eyes playfully and confess.

"Fiiiine," I say like spilling this secret is torturous, but we both know I've always been happy to share everything with her.

Having my parents is like having a cool boss - they're fun, but they're still your boss until you quit, and then you can be friends. Graduating high school was me quitting, and ever since then, we've been more friends than anything. It's a gift I know I'm lucky to have, and I don't know how I would have made it this far without them.

"I met a guy at McNamara's on my first day after the library. They accidentally switched our subs and we started talking. He's here from England for work. He appraises things, so we both love history, and we're both here to learn more about the lighthouse and this area. So, yes, we went to The Broken Mast," I add, and she gestures for me to go on while she eats her soup. "His name is Theo, and there's just something about him. I don't know...it's like I've met him before, but I know I haven't. That's weird, I know."

"The universe is a weird place, hun. Right place, right time," she nods without an ounce of judgement in her voice. "You were meant to eat his hoagie - wait - no."

It's too late to take back her Freudian slip, and in seconds, we're both giggling and jabbing each other with our elbows, threatening to spill our chicken noodle soup. At the sound of our cackling, the bedroom door opens and Dad walks in to take in the sight before him.

"No boys allowed in the pillow fort?" he says with a laugh, his expression telling us both that he might have heard enough to know what we're talking about. The way Mom melts when she sees him, and the added softness to his eyes, reminds me of how badly I want a love like theirs one day. She tilts her head in invitation, and he comes over to the opposite side of the bed to sit next to her on top of the comforter. Taking the bowl from her hands, he laces his fingers with hers.

"Mom was just telling me how good of a caretaker you are for her. Sounds like you're a better night nurse than an actual night nurse," I tease playfully, but the expression on his face isn't one of adoration - it's complete and utter confusion. Sharing a look with Mom, who seems to be getting sleepier by the second with all the energy she must have spent earlier, I meet his eyes again. Lowering my voice, I elaborate to show him I know so he doesn't have to play Captain Oblivious. "The moonlight serenades and midnight snuggles are cute, Dad, it's ok."

"Even if you do mess up the covers, I still love it, babe," Mom nudges his shoulder and he creases his brows.

"Sorry to disappoint my favorite girls, but I've been keeping the couch warm," he admits, and a wave of unease tingles its way through my body all the way down to the tips of my fingers. Sensing the odd silence that's settled over the room like a fog, he rushes to lighten the mood as Mom settles farther down in the bed. Her smile never fades as she stares up at him even when sleep threatens to pull her under already. "Wait, in this fever dream, am I Dr. Steamy or Dr. Dreamy?"

"Hmmmm always Dr. Steamy," she answers, pretending it was a tough call, but we both know who her favorite is. Dad tucks her in as she closes her eyes, nodding to me that it's time to leave so she can get more rest. Without being asked, he grabs both empty bowls and I follow him into the kitchen as he deposits them into the sink, heading for the door.

Before I get the chance to speak, he's calling my name as he walks outside toward the lighthouse. I rush to follow him, my heart jumping in anticipation that the steps might finally be finished and I can see inside. I've been doing my best not to rush him, especially since it unexpectedly became a solo project, but I can't deny the sensation that it calls to me. The more I research it, the closer I feel to it.

Standing in front of the lighthouse in the late afternoon is a surreal moment. Stopping at its base and looking up, it's like it was built to touch the sky; a maritime Tower of Babel. Time has been selective with the white color of it, but whatever its been through, it wears the centuries like battle scars. As I reach my hand out to touch the side of it, I close my eyes as if I can feel the link to every year before this one.

"You comin'?" Dad calls, catching my attention and severing me from the connection I didn't realize I'd been lost in. He's standing in the doorway of the lighthouse, proudly at the top of the small set of stairs that he finished. I feel my feet move toward him, but I can't fight the sensation that I'm paddle boating with a current - my effort to move is unnecessary because it's pulling me with it.

Placing my hand in his, I climb the wooden steps and cross the threshold with him into Corlucius Lighthouse. The moment we step inside, we're instantly shaken by the door slamming behind us, the sound echoing upward. My eyes follow the soundwaves as my gaze travels around the red spiral staircase up to the darkness at the top. The interior walls are a stark match for the outside with worn paint and exposed brick. The sound decrescendos to silence like a pin drop in an endless cavern.

I'm not sure what I was expecting when I stepped foot into this structure, but while Dad fidgets with various checks on paint and assesses the restoration at hand, I crease my brow as I stare at the top. The eerie wave of familiarity travels through my veins like a slowly dripping poison, and I try to make sense of where I've seen it before. The oddest feeling wraps around me to hold me here, waiting for me to see what it wants to show me. *I bet I've seen it in the countless photos and articles I dug up, or the clips from Destination Restoration I watched on the plane ride here.*

A small noise turns my attention back to my dad, who is leaning against the wall and intently watching me. He opens his mouth and closes it, like he's trying to find the right way to say something. Mom is the one with the words, and Dad is the one with the handy man hands, so whatever it is, I can tell it's probably something he'd prefer Mom say - like when it was time for "the talk" and buying my first tampons.

"What's up?" I ask, breaking the silence and giving him safe passage from the awkward war of the words he's having in his mind. His shoulders instantly relax, and I can tell whatever is on his mind has been weighing on him for longer than today.

"You know you can talk to us, right? Not just Mom. I'm here for you too, kiddo," he says with a shrug. When he sees my eyes narrow in confusion, he sighs at the fact he'll have to elaborate on something he doesn't want to. "I know you moved out here fast and went through a lot before that, just...you know...if you need to talk to someone, we love you...it kills me to hear you fight with it every night."

"I'm fine really. I promise," I reassure him. "I know I've been freaking out a little lately, but it's just being in a new place and a little anxiety. I've been doing much better though, see?" I do a little spin to ease a smirk out of him, but when I reach his eyes, there's nothing but concern.

"You're not even sleeping through the night. I can hear you pacing, and I hate hearing you cry. Mom and I just want you to be ok and know we're here for you," he answers with a pained expression in the soft wrinkles around his eyes.

"Dad, really. I've been sleeping fine, and I'm not even upset about what Marcus did anymore. He's probably tried calling, but like you said, he can't reach me here. I feel fine, and I was over him the second I found out he cheated. Maybe it's just the way the old house sounds at night. It's not me though," I say with a shrug and look back up at the top of the spiral stairs. "Theo says they make all kinds of-"

"-Theo?" Dad asks with a slightly out of character voice, no longer masking his concern. "Who is that?"

"He's someone I met in town actually. We're both working on projects right now, but mine's for school and he's an appraiser, so he's working with a client in town. He's funny and really nice, and he's from England. You know I've always loved-" I start, but my words are interrupted as my dad's facial expression morphs into something else I can't place. He moves from the relaxed pose against the wall to a tall stance with his arms crossed over his chest.

"Sounds like he's looking for an easy distraction while he's docked, kiddo. You don't need two broken hearts so quickly. He'll use you and go back home to whoever is waiting for him there. That's how they are. That's how they always are. You need to focus on what we have going on here. We need you here."

His words are sharp, even if unintentionally, and now I know why Mom is the one who handles the tough talks with me. Apparently, Dad trying to be concerned is like a toddler running with scissors. When the hurt flashes across my cheeks like a freshly throbbing slap, the part that makes me mad is that he doesn't instantly take back his words.

"I've been here, and when I'm not, I'm grabbing Mom cough syrup and anything I can. I'm not choosing Theo over her," I clarify with my hands out in a show of surrender.

"Still had time for a date though," he mumbles and it's so uncharacteristically passive aggressive that I can't let it go. The sound of my frustration bounces itself off the walls like a bullet.

"I've spent the same amount of time in town that you have in a 6-pack of beer and a box of cigars. I was really excited about being in this lighthouse, Dad, but you're being really unfair. Let's do this later. I'm tired," I say, doing my best to deescalate the situation before I say something out of hurt.

Before he can say anything, I walk out of the lighthouse and back down the freshly finished stairs back to the keeper's house. I don't turn for confirmation that he's following me to apologize. I know he owes me one, but right now I'm in defensive mode and all I want to do is seek reassurance that he's not right from the one person who can quell the silent storm in my heart.

CHAPTER FOURTEEN

ODESSA

Looking down at my phone, I hover my thumb over Theo's name. I'm barely in my bedroom as the sun begins to set, casting a warm glow on the walls. Closing the door behind me, the desk chair calls to me. I can't think of a more desirable way to spend the evening than to hopefully talk to Theo and watch the moon appear over the sea. Approaching the desk chair like it's a long lost lover, I almost face-plant when I trip over the carpet in the center of the room again.

Righting myself, I lean down to fix the dog-eared corner of it. I can't help but curse my own two left feet every time I walk around this room for some reason. Maybe as part of the restoration we can donate this troublesome area rug to another room. I'd move it now if it wasn't for my intense desire to be as authentic as possible when I complete my project. Sitting at the wooden desk chair, I look at the small candle poised on the brass candle holder standing guard in the window.

Holding my phone, I stumble through the labyrinth of my thoughts as I attempt to find the right thing to say. From needing to make sure I'm not just a fling to avoiding facing why it would bother me if I was, all I know is I need a palate cleanser from talking to my dad. Before I can compose and delete a text ten times over, my phone vibrates in my hands. Looking down, I smile at the welcome notification, the insecurity placed in the back of my mind dissipating.

Theo: Let me take you out to dinner tomorrow, Dess.

Me: Wish I could, but I promised Mom I'd make her favorite.

Theo: And what would that be?

Me: Chicken parm and garlic knots.

Theo: Count me in.

Me: My parents will be here. Is that too much for you? It's ok if you don't want to.

Theo: Count me in, Dess. I'd love to.

Theo: Can't say no to a homemade meal - or to you.

Me: I wouldn't want you to say no either. Missing my chicken parm is illegal in all 50 states. I didn't know if you knew that.

Theo: Well I can't quite argue with that now can I? Sweet dreams. X

Me: You too, Theo. X

At first I was slightly nervous that the brief conversation escalated into a "meet the parents" dinner, but it only makes me feel more confident that he's not just filling his spare time with me. The more the idea settles in, the more I convince myself that once Dad meets him, he'll see it too. Theo and I may have just begun, but it feels significant. I don't know why yet, but it does. I already know Mom will love him, but I don't foresee her making an overnight recovery. At least Dad will see that I'm in good hands - really nice, vein-defined hands. My mind takes a delicious detour to one of the first parts of Theo I noticed.

Basking in the warmth of the memory of his kiss, I miss the two short rings of an incoming call. I don't get the chance to answer before it stops, and the balloon of hope in my chest deflates when I see it's not Theo. It's just another unknown spam call, and with that, I yawn. Although I'd planned on taking another bite out of my project, the events of the day must be wearing on me. I decide to change into my sushi print pajamas and call it an early night. *More beauty sleep before a big date can't hurt, right?*

***

I can't see anything in the darkness. It feels like I'm everywhere and nowhere, dropped and suspended into an endless abyss where time doesn't exist. I can't see anything aside from myself, but I can smell the salt of the sea in the breeze that touches my body like a gentle and careful lover. I feel safe, but know it could be fleeting.

Suddenly in the distance, I hear it. The faintest of melodies threaded in between the rumbles of a far away thunder storm. I'm waiting for it to return to me, but I don't know what it is. There's nothing but the darkness that lacks a measurable depth, the muffled sounds of a song in a storm, and the longing ache in my heart.

Thinking of my heart, I hold my hand over my chest. It feels like it's cracking open to share my loss with the world before it swallows me whole. It's when I realize that the darkness I'm shrouded in is heartbreak that I feel it begin to consume me until there's nothing left but hopelessness. I'm lost in it. Drowning in the coldest waters of grief is where I lost the will to wade water. It's where I've come to the realization that I am not to be saved from this fate - that the end of my torment is undoubtedly nigh. The only power I have left is the choice of when.

Looking up, I see the familiar spot where the spiral staircase meets the ceiling. I can't breathe. I can't breathe.

***

I jolt awake, shooting straight up into a seated position and grasp at my throat to claw the air into my lungs. I feel like I haven't been breathing, and with the cold sweat on my back, I come to the understanding that although insanely vivid, it was only a nightmare. As if that could reassure me, knowing it wasn't real, a chilling setting becomes clearer by the second.

My hand still over my chest to feel my heart rate, I take in my surroundings as I do my best to ground myself with each breath. *In through your nose, and out through your mouth. Head to the north, then head to the south.* I repeat the phrase to myself as my mom did when I would get overwhelmed as a kid. My heart rages against its enclosure anyway, beating at the ribbed bars for freedom. Holding the railing of the spiral stairs, I shakily stand to find that the only light sources are the newly installed emergency light on the wall next to me and the moonlight that shines onto the grass outside the opened door.

The sound of footsteps pattering down the stairs startles me, holding my attention and steeling my spine. I'm no longer able to blame the wind or the stress of Marcus because what I hear is undeniable. There is someone coming down the lighthouse's spiral stairs, and the pace is quickening to match my pulse. The glow of the emergency light only illuminates two or three wraps of the winding staircase, but above that, it's sheer darkness. The footsteps move quicker, the sound coming closer to me.

"D-Dad?" I ask out loud.

The steps pause, and I can't tell if they stop because I'm right or because I'm wrong. *If that's not Dad, then who is in here with me in the middle of the night?* The silence stretches from seconds to a minute, and the rational side of my brain finally becomes louder than the adrenaline-induced freeze I'd been locked into. Just as an iota of tension leaves my body through the unclenching of my jaw, the steps begin again, only this time, with a speedy purpose. Based on the clinking of the metal stairs, if I don't leave the lighthouse now, whoever it is will step directly into the emergency light any second now, and I don't know if that's a relief or a reason to run.

Before I can decide what the best course of action is, my fight or flight kicks in choosing flight, and I turn quickly toward the open door as the steps pound behind me, echoing up the walls above. With four rushed strides, I'm in the doorway and I know if I just had the guts to turn around, I'd be face-to-face with my midnight mystery maritime companion, but I don't.

Just as I reach for the door, the footsteps run toward me, and they're so close I know I'm in arm's reach. In an instant, I'm jolted back by my neck as something travels through my body as if I'm not even there.

Heavier than a breeze, but lighter than fog, the wind rushes through and around me as if it wanted to race me outside. Fighting my way back into my conscious body, I gather my strength and run out of the lighthouse and down the steps.

I don't even set both bare feet on the grass before the door of the lighthouse slams shut, the sound like a shotgun in the once peaceful silence of the night. I risk the glance back and find there's nothing there but the door. Standing on the grass, bathed in moonlight and wearing the sleep tank and shorts I remember putting on after texting Theo, my eyes adjust and I look around.

When my eyes pass the keeper's house and land on the dock at the rocky edge, I'm frozen again. *No.* When I blink hard, it doesn't go away. Standing there with an outstretched hand in my direction is a shadowy male figure. I shake my head again and slowly start to walk toward the house, but as I take a step, so does he.

My survival mode fully kicking in, I hold my breath and sprint as fast as I can into the house without looking back to see if I was followed. I throw the lock on the kitchen door, and rush up to my room taking two steps at a time without a care in the world that I might awaken my parents. At this rate, I wouldn't care if I woke up the entire mainland. *I can't let Marcus get away with finding me here.*

The moment I'm back in my room safely, I grab my phone from the nightstand, ripping the charger from it and rushing to the window. If I get a photo of him on the island, I can prove he's in violation of his restraining order. I race to the window and open the camera only to find the dock completely empty again and no one there. A lone tear escapes my eye, and the crash from my adrenaline pulls me to the unmade bed I must have wandered from in my sleep.

As I lay back in my bed, I let the night's events sink in to bring clarity and rationality to it all. Sorting and overanalyzing my thoughts and memories, a few things become very clear to me. One, whoever has been showing up at the dock can't be Marcus because he would need a boat to get here, and there's nothing out there but ours. Two, what happened in the lighthouse feels beyond logical explanation. I don't know if I have any beliefs to challenge, but there's something happening here I need help making sense of. I need to know what's happening to me when I'm here.

When I think about what I can do to seek out the answers I desperately need, my cloudy mind clears and one person remains. As I do my best to control the shaking in my hands that has yet to fade, I send one text before I let sleep take me under.

Chapter Fifteen

Theodore

Waking up to the smell of freshly brewed coffee every morning has been a welcome delight to my stay. When I promised Mum and Greta that I'd live the authentic experience here, I fully expected quite the opposite when I'd seen the weather-worn exterior of the Victorian home. Once I stepped foot onto the hand-woven mat outside the door, I've spent each day with an increasingly odd feeling of belonging. I fully intend on blaming the coffee and its ability to keep me awake after the dreams plaguing me with restless nights.

With a stretch, the sheets fall to my bare waist and I reach for my phone on the nightstand. My brows crease when I see the text notification, not because it's from Dessa - I quite like that part - it's the fact that the message was sent at 3am.

I narrow my eyes as I think more about the text that seems nothing at all like the Dessa I kissed on the dock. Allowing myself a moment while my whole body responds to the memory of her lips on mine, I impulsively touch her name on my phone's screen to call her. Clearing my throat, I take a swig of the water on my nightstand to wash down the sleep from my voice. She answers quickly, not allowing the phone to ring more than once.

"Hey," she says, sounding instantly relieved, and I can't fight the way her tone is quickly beginning to worry me. I do my best to keep it casual, and if she wants to open up to me, I'll let her.

"And to you. I got your text. I'm scheduled to stop by today, so why don't I bring you along with me and you can ask her whatever you'd like. Unless you'd rather me just ask while I'm there if you're not coming to town today," I offer, doing my damn best to hide the fact that I can tell something is off.

"Well, actually, I'm already here. Not here as in your place, I mean at the coffee shop. You know Beachy Beans? I guess I couldn't sleep and just came in early...figured I'd wait here until the library opened," she trails off.

"I know the place. I'll be there soon. A coffee sounds great," I say, and truthfully so. She gives a small thanks before hanging up, and I slip out of the sheets to shower. I might not have to report to the Goodman's home for a few hours, but my sense of urgency is still ever present. Something is wrong and Dessa needs my help. That's the loudest thought in my mind as I rush through my morning routine and grab my messenger bag on the way out.

One of the benefits of a small town is that everything is within walking distance for the most part, and coincidentally Beachy Beans is one of the closer spots to where I'm staying. I'm able to make my way there in less than ten minutes, but mostly because I jogged until

I could see the shop. As soon as the soft blue building on the corner was in eye shot, I slow my pace to a brisk walk as not to alarm her if she can see me from her seat.

Walking into the quaint little coffee shop, I see her waiting in a corner bistro table next to the window. She's in leggings and a college hoodie, even though it's not really cool out. The moment she sees me, her tense shoulders relax and she practically leaps into a hug when I reach the table. When her arms wrap around my neck, her scent circles around me like a coiled blanket, I drop my messenger bag in the empty chair to put one hand in her chocolate wavy hair and the other on her back. I can feel her body soften in my hold as protectiveness surges through me unexpectedly. If I could exist in any other form, I'd become armor to keep her safe from whatever has her damn near trembling as she molds easily into my chest. In the back of my mind, I worry she can hear the way my heart races with her against me.

Slowly separating, we sit at the small table and let a brief silence pass, not knowing who should talk first. Without a word, she slides a small coffee mug to me before picking up another to take a sip. I look at the mug and its contents. She ordered me a coffee and she knew what I'd like. The realization that she knew I'd like my coffee black paired with ordering for me would have made me smile if I wasn't so concerned about her. I put one hand around the warm blue mug, and the other I place gently on top of hers.

"Dessa, talk to me. What's happened?" I ask, lowering my tone and tracing small circles on the back of her hand. She stares at the motion and a glassiness coats her eyes. "You can tell me."

"I know this is going to sound crazy, and I feel like I'm going crazy just saying it out loud, but...I, umm, well," she struggles. "I think there's something going on on the island. I'm...experiencing things...things that don't make sense."

She fidgets with her hair and takes a sip of her coffee, but I thoroughly enjoy that she doesn't move the hand that rests under my own. I take the first gulp of my coffee as well and it's exactly what I would have ordered for myself. I don't know how she knows the smallest details about me without my telling her, but she does, and the comfort it brings me feels foreign but welcome. Black. Two Sugars.

"Don't think about how it sounds," I reassure her. "I promise it won't sound crazy."

"I think the island is possessed," Dessa instantly blurts like it's an embarrassing secret she has to say in one quick breath before losing her confidence. She looks at me, likely expecting me to flinch or show signs of judgement, but when I slowly nod, she continues. "What I mean is, I think there's something happening that exists beyond explanation, and if you knew me better you'd know how hard that is for me to admit. It seems impossible when I think about it."

"I don't think it's impossible, it's quite common actually," I say, and she looks at me in disbelief. "You love history, yes? Haven't you ever stopped to touch something and felt it? It's what interested me in pursuing a career of these sorts of appraisals - the ability to hold hundreds of years in my hands...Mum and my sis, Greta, they believe in traces left behind. They're entirely superstitious."

"That's it?" she asks with an exhale topped with a slight giggle. "You just believe me? Just like that?"

"Would you rather me tell you it was just the wind or that you're just overworked and stressed, and you've allowed it to manifest into hallucinations that are both visual and auditory?" I ask as I sip my coffee. I can't help the slight smirk we share, and the warmth I feel that isn't just from my mug.

"That was always the part of horror movies I hated," she admits, running her hand through her waves as my eyes track the way her eyes shine behind her tortoise shell glasses. "You know the part, right? The girl sees a ghost and tells the leading man just for him to write it off and make her question herself. And then of course, she's right and they're in danger because he didn't just trust her instincts. Classic."

"Greta hates that too. She always - wait, so you think of me as your leading man?" I tease, and I wish I could paint the entire world the rosy shade of her cheeks when she meets my gaze. I wiggle my eyebrows at her just to hear the heavenly sound of her laughter because even as soft as it is, it's still completely disarming.

"Theo, focus," Dessa says with the snap of her fingers. Her hands have stopped trembling, and she seems more at ease with every curl of her lips. "And...thank you for not thinking I'm crazy. I've never experienced anything like this."

"I haven't, save for the dreams," I admit without thinking and she inhales a small gasp. Realizing I've been more open than I initially intended, I explain. "I'm certain it's just our research and my work, but I can't lie. I've been having vivid dreams that I'm on a ship in a storm, then lost at sea. I haven't thought much of it since I used to have recurring dreams of dark water as a school boy, but it seems they've reappeared since I've gotten settled in here."

"That sounds really scary," she says and I shrug it off. I grew up being afraid, but the swimming lessons Mum pushed me to sign up for helped cure my fear of the unknown. She also banned shark movies until I was sixteen.

"Nightmares are no match for the leading man," I answer with bravado and an exaggerated puffed out chest just to watch her playfully roll her eyes. "But, I've texted the Goodmans, and Sarah said we could stop by whenever we're ready. I think you'll find her to be very open-minded, and she'll be able to tell you more. She'll love you actually."

Just looking at Dessa while I taste the impulsively spoken word on my tongue makes me long for the feeling of her hair tangled in between my fingers and her soft lips on mine. It takes everything in me to ignore the earth shattering feeling I get when I'm in her orbit, but I do - for the sake of her needing my help.

***

Sitting at the Goodman's dining room table for the past hour as I listen to Dessa recount every detail of what's been happening to her family on Corlucius Island, I do my best not to feign concern. One bowl of Sarah's famous homemade clam chowder and two biscuits later, the room is quiet,

"Well well darling, your parents' renovations must be kicking up the old spirits," Sarah concludes as she pats her gray curls. "My nana always warned me about how those things can happen. You know this whole island is full of history, and a lot of that history is bound and determined to tell its side whether the living like it or not."

"Do you know anything about who lived there before we did?" Dessa asks, sipping her lemonade and stealing grateful glances at me when she can. "Or what we can do to, well, help them move on?"

"Not so keen on sharing your house? Imagine how they must feel," Sarah chuckles. Stirring her soup, she continues. "There's not some magic spell or sage to use that's going to make them see the light, dear. They're not there to scare you, they're there for your help. Ever heard your parents tell you that bees are more afraid of you than you are of them? Well, spirits are the same way. They wait for us to notice what they're trying to tell us or show us."

"So...if Dessa can figure out what they want, it'll stop?" I ask.

"Who's to say? It's not up to us to evict the spirits before us. We should learn from them instead. Maybe whoever it is trusts you, Dessa. The previous owners didn't report anything. The next time anything happens, remember that. Ask for a message, and in the meantime you both should be more careful to observe some of our little rituals," Sarah explains. When Dessa and I exchange glances, Sarah senses the confusion. "You have a lot to learn, kids, but at least remember the most important one - if there's a storm, you lay a flower along shore to honor any love the sea has taken. That's what my nana taught me."

As Sarah tells Dess about any other stories she can remember, I try not to stare at Dessa's natural beauty or the delightfully adorable way she bites her lip when she's thinking really hard. I can tell she's going to immediately put this theory to the test when we're not in the presence of the Goodmans.

Once we wrap up the impromptu meeting with Mrs. Goodman, it's lunchtime, and I walk Dessa back to the pier where her boat waits. It's a quiet walk for most of it, both of us processing everything we'd learned. When we stop at the pier in front of her small boat, she turns to me and she's so close I could press my lips to hers if I just leaned forward ever so slightly.

"Is is stupid to be a little scared to go back?" Dessa asks honestly as she looks up to me, wrapping her arms around my neck in a move that feels equally as comfortable as exciting, like we're new and old to each other at the same time.

"Not at all," I answer as I tuck a rogue chocolate curl behind her ear and under the arm of her glasses. "Anything out of the ordinary can be frightening, but the adventure of discovery is what makes people like us seek it out. I have a feeling you're probably more daring than I am."

"We'll have to put it to the test tonight then. Dinner?" Dessa reminds me with a slight tilt of her head into my hand and I shamelessly melt a little more.

"No unseen force could keep me away from a home-cooked meal," I say with a laugh. Of course the idea of chicken parmesan sounds delicious, but I can't deny that the idea of her cooking a meal she loves for me isn't utterly appealing.

A gust of wind gently nudges her body towards mine ever so slightly, and it's the only cue I need from the universe to give into the desire I can't seem to shake ever since I've been in her presence. I caress my thumbs along her cheeks as I surrender myself to the inexplicable magnetism we have. Leaning down to her, I feel her use her hold around my neck to bring her body to mine, and I can barely keep from moaning into her mouth. My lips brush hers softly at first, but in a moment as my tongue seeks entry, the need for more escalates. Her teeth nip at my bottom lip, and I fight the buckle of my knees. I'm not even ashamed to admit the ways I would let her ruin me just to build me in any image or likeness she desired.

I kiss her like I'll never see her again and she returns the sentiment tenfold, making it difficult to pry my lips from hers, but when the wind picks up again, wrapping us in our own small gentle cyclone, we know we should hurry. Separating our lips only to rest our foreheads against each other, our breathing is matched and heavy. It's hard to imagine I've ever truly cared for anyone if this is what it's meant to feel like.

"We'd better go," Dessa whispers, the warmth of her breath on my lips where I can still feel her kiss.

"Yes. Yes, I know," I whisper back, pulling away just enough to run my hands down her arms to lace my fingers with hers. "Let's get you home."

Chapter Sixteen

Odessa

The boat ride back to Corlucius Island was choppy, but having Theo's arms wrapped around me from behind gave me a sense of security I haven't felt in a long time. I know he's still new in my life, but oddly, it doesn't feel that way at all. How can I feel so comfortable with someone I've known for less than a month when being with Marcus for years never brought me this level of inner peace?

As we tie the boat and step all the way onto the dock, I wait for him to react to the picturesque view like I had, but when I make eye contact, he's only staring at me. When our eyes meet, so do our hands, and with the pull of the wind, the world around us drifts away. All I can see are his lips framed by the shadow of his dark stubble, and the way he looks at my mouth like all he wants to do is make me his. I feel like I already am, like I've never belonged to anyone else before this. He leans down slightly and I part my lips to welcome his kiss, but the sound of rushed steps and a familiar frantic voice interrupts the moment.

"Odessa, where have you been? I've been calling you for an hour," Dad says as he marches up to us quickly, holding his phone up to me so I can see the missed calls. I pull my phone out from my purse, but I show nothing on the call log.

"My phone didn't ring. What's wrong?" I ask, noticing his unusual demeanor. He looks nervous, restless, and full of concern. He doesn't even acknowledge Theo standing next to me, or the fact that he hasn't let go of my hand.

"It's your mom. She went to the kitchen to get something to drink and she fainted. When she came to, she got into another one of her coughing spells and there was some blood. I called you because I need the boat to take her to the hospital. I want someone to look at her," he recounts, anxiously running his hands through his hair.

"We can go with you," I offer, but he puts a hand up and shakes his head.

"I need someone on the property. You can stay here, kiddo, but I'm taking Mom with me. We shouldn't be gone too long, just please be careful and stay put," Dad says, but he stresses the last part a little too much for my comfort. *When he says to be careful, does he mean in general or does he know that something else is happening that escapes logic?*

"We will," I agree, and it's at that moment he realizes I'm not alone. Looking Theo up and down, I can't decipher the look he gives him. "Dad, this is Theo."

"Pleasure to meet you, sir. I only wish it would have been on better terms," Theo says, separating from me and holding his hand out to my Dad who thankfully shakes it much to my relief. I'm sure Theo will get the full inquisition from both of my parents, but for now, Dad's priority is getting to the mainland so Mom can see a doctor.

"Keep her safe," my dad commands quietly to Theo in almost a whisper. Theo nods in return, giving a wordless yes from one protector to another. Before I have the chance to say anything, Mom walks across the dock to us holding her overnight bag and wearing a light blue tracksuit.

"Mom," I say in almost a plea as I reach for the bag she's carrying. It's much lighter than I thought, which only establishes how weak she's become. In the daylight, she looks drained and pale. Dad rushes to her side to help her aboard the small boat, turning to me as he pulls me into a hug.

"Be careful here...please," he quietly says into my hair causing fear to creep back under my skin, goosebumps prickling my arms. When he backs up, the look in his eyes isn't just concern for Mom - it's for me too. Something has him spooked, and I'm almost certain I know what it is. With a kiss to the top of my head, he hops onto the boat and speeds off to Clarkston, leaving Theo and I on the dock with his comforting arm around my shoulders.

***

"You were right. That chicken parmesan was the best I've ever tasted. You're an incredible chef," Theo praises as he stretches his arms over his head. I can't stop my eyes from traveling down his button up shirt that tightens at his chest. Clocking my distraction, he grins like the cheshire cat as my cheeks flush with interest and a hint of embarrassment.

"I'm glad you enjoyed it," I say as I stand to clear our plates from the oak kitchen table. As I reach for his plate, he puts a hand over mine, and I feel the warmth of his touch all the way to my toes.

"Let me," he asserts as he stands. I let go of the plate as he takes it, and the one out of my hands. I follow him as he walks to the sink to rinse them off. Standing next to him at the sink in this empty kitchen feels so normal and domestic, even if it's a big step in every other relationship. It feels like such a small normalcy to me.

I open my mouth to speak when my phone vibrates on the table, sending a buzzing sound throughout the silence of the house and we both jump. Realizing how on edge we both are, we share a small laugh and I reach for the phone. I read the text out loud.

> Dad: Hey kiddo, they're going to run some tests and keep Mom under observation for now. Looks like we won't be back so soon. You and your friend stay put. Be careful.

> Me: Theo and I will be here if you or Mom need anything. Love u

> Dad: Love u 2

As the evening turns to night, I finish the full tour of the property so Theo knows his way around. I catch him looking at a few things harder than usual, like he's searching for a ghost or a clue, but nothing makes itself known. It's almost like when you call the help desk for a computer issue just for the computer not to replicate the problem, suddenly Theo's presence means nothing unusual happens. His trained eye seemingly catalogs his surroundings and I suddenly remember his profession.

"Are there things here that hold a lot of value?" I casually ask, not because I have any interest in convincing my parents to sell it, but because I'm curious at what defines monetary value as time passes. Every morsel of insight his expertise can lend could be invaluable to my research. "How do you even determine something like that? I'd have a hard time separating sentimental value from actual value in a place like this."

We stop in the small room that my father is certain was a study or a living room as the window perfectly frames the entrance to the lighthouse not too far away. Theo surveys everything from floor to ceiling like he's in a museum with an eye for value and appreciation equally.

"I know what you mean, Dess. This place is…"

"Surreal?" I offer as he trails off. Whatever word he's looking for, I know it, but we can't put it adequately into a sentence. "Like a portal between then and now? Maybe that's what triggered the dreams. Honestly, the longer you're here while nothing happens, the more I think you should have just said it was the wind."

He shares my laugh, but the smile doesn't reach its full beam as our eyes meet in the dimly lit study. The wind has picked up and darkness has settled gently around the island like we're being tucked into bed. *Bed*. Just the thought of it with Theo inches away from me makes my body respond.

"Maybe it is, or maybe the leading man scared the spookies away," he says, straightening up his spine and puffing out his chest in a show of exaggerated masculinity. "Or maybe they just can't scare you as much as the potential to break your leg tripping over these."

I roll my eyes playfully, as I look through the boxes on the floor. They're filled with blueprints, paint swatches, permits, and other papers that my parents have collected during the renovation. One box is only full of various odds and ends that look like they belong in my dad's toolbox. Theo flips the lid on another and lifts an amber bottle into the light.

"I knew it," I say like a detective holding the smoking gun evidence. "I knew he was drinking more than just a couple beers."

"Not from this one. It's unopened," Theo reveals with a nostalgic grin as he spins the bottle to examine the label. "It's actually my mum's favorite whiskey. Ironically, it was also my first drink."

"Your first drink was a shot? I think I like your mother already," I laugh. Just the thought of a young Theo's face after the unforgettable initial burn of a strong shot. Feeling a little relieved at the lack of a haunted house, my relaxed nerves seem to hone in on the beautiful man in front of me. "We could do one together."

"Oh yeah?" He says, his tone transforming into a flirtatious challenge. "Ladies first."

He hands me the bottle of whiskey, allowing our fingers to brush as I grasp the neck. It's only for the briefest of moments, but the touch of any part of his skin on mine causes liquid fire to course through my veins. I unscrew the cap and slowly bring the bottle to my lips as Theo watches me intently, his eyes rotating from lips back to my gaze. The smooth whiskey goes down my throat leaving a path of soft heat in its wake, and I exhale a hot breath that feels like it should be on fire. I use the back of my hand to wipe the remaining drop that clings to my lips, and I hand the bottle back to him.

Taking it from me, he throws back his shot fairly quickly. He leaves his eyes closed like he's watching a movie I can't see, then exhales just as I did - long and slow. Putting the bottle down on the small table near the window, he turns back to me. Without saying a word to each other, the unspoken admission permeates the air around us. Like the magnets we are, we're pulled back toward each other as the lights flicker above us.

We look out the window as if we can see the wind from the sound it makes, and when we turn back to each other, the weighted truth sits between our bodies. His hand slowly slides around my waist to rest at the small of my back, pulling me toward him softly but with an unmistakable and purposeful intention. His other hand gently journeys from my wrist up my arm and my shoulder to rest on the side of my jaw, his thumb caressing my bottom lip like a feather.

Theo touches me like I'm an artifact he's appraising, like I'm a delicate yet priceless relic that holds the secrets of history beneath my skin. The look in his eyes tells me he wants to kiss me, to destroy me for anyone else, but he doesn't - he's as lost in my gaze as I am in his. I don't know how much time passes, but it feels faster and slower at the same time, like time itself has paused its never ending gears to bear witness to our connection. As his thumb presses down, my lips part. On instinct, the tip of my tongue moves to taste him.

At the motion, his eyes darken as the lights flicker once more at the beating of the wind, the house creaking as it withstands nature's battery. He slides in farther, and my lips wrap completely around his thumb down to the knuckle. Letting out a small moan as he watches me, I know what he's thinking because I'm thinking it too. As if our energy is draining everything in the house, suddenly the power blinks and all clocks beep, but we haven't moved. Sliding his wet thumb out of my mouth, he uses it to caress my cheek, and every cell in my body electrifies.

"Theo," I plead in a whisper, but for what I don't know. Everything. All of it. All of him.

"Dessa," he responds, right before he pulls my mouth to his in a kiss that slices the tether to my sanity.

CHAPTER SEVENTEEN

THEODORE

My kiss as a tidal wave crashing onto the rocks of her lips, I can't think of anything except how holding her in my arms feels like home. It's a foreign sensation to me, and one I never knew I so desperately needed to become complete. How could I have spent another day on this orbiting rock without knowing what this brand of comfort could truly be?

I'm unable to pull myself from the sheer awe of this perfect woman as my arm snakes around her waist even tighter and my kiss deepens. The walls creak and my soul cracks open at the sound she makes when my tongue pushes further into her mouth. Her arms that have been at her side until now wrap around my neck, anchoring us to each other through the tempest that rages within us. The moment she pulls the back of my hair, I groan into her mouth, and I swear I can feel it vibrate down her spine as she pushes her body into mine.

Without breaking the seal of my lips on hers, I allow my hands to generously wander down her sides to the soft round seat of her ass. Dessa's body responds to every inch I touch, and when I grab and lift, she wraps her legs around my waist like she was always meant to. We can barely take a moment to breathe as I pull back to make sure I don't trip over the boxes in the room. Something about laying her down on the floor here doesn't feel right to me, although at this point, I'd settle for anywhere as long as I could make her truly mine in every way imaginable.

Lights surge in the house as I carefully hold her in my arms while taking step by step to the second floor until we reach the threshold of her bedroom. The relief that her parents won't be returning tonight is palpable, and it's a blessing I'll never be able to repay. Walking over a few piles of paper on the floor, I kick the upturned corner of the carpet before gently laying her on the small bed in the corner of the room facing the window. She doesn't have a lot of light in here, but it's enough to see each other and the look of desire we both share equally.

As a chill travels through the room, I drag us under the blankets and settle on top of her in between her thighs. In between frantic kisses, we pull at our clothes like every thread is in the way of what has always meant to be. Every garment between us is too far apart. Dessa helps me pull my shirt over my head as I drag her leggings off of her trembling legs. My pants and her hoodie are last to go until we're in the final barriers that separate us from seeing every part of each other.

"Are you sure?" I ask as I kiss the tops of her shoulders where the straps of her soft pink cotton bra sit like a bookmark on my favorite page. She nods as she pulls my mouth back to hers, and I trace the straps with my fingertips before guiding them down her arms and unhooking the back.

With her bare to me save for her matching panties, I inhale the warm comforting scent that lives between her neck and shoulder - a mix of home and the sea, of hope and lust. In that breath, I give part of myself to her, allowing a small surrender to this moment even if it never happens again. As I'm trapped in the fear of never knowing her like this again, she tilts her hips upward toward mine and I understand completely what she's silently asking of me.

Hooking my fingers into the sides of her panties, I drag them down her thighs, the small strand of glistening arousal connecting them to her until I pull them to her knees and off of her ankles. I'm frozen at the sight of her laid bare before me on this bed looking at me like she can see the darkest parts of my heart where I hide my insecurities, my guilt, and my pain. My vulnerability is matched, and as I slide my briefs off, I know we're equals in this now. We see each other for every bit of who we are, who we want to be, and who we were.

Unable to stand one more moment without touching her, I lower myself back down, letting the heat of our bodies sear us together from the bottom up. Her thighs part to welcome me as close as I can be, and my hardened length nudges her drenched core, pulling a sudden inhale from her lips. She might be bracing herself for my entry, but even as impatient as some parts of me feel right now, all I want to do is take my time.

With a slight curl of my hips to tease her, I push at her entrance before sliding my body lower. Bringing my lips back to her collarbone, I lay a trail of kisses down to the most perfect breasts I've ever seen in my life. I may not have seen a lot from my teens to my thirties, having only dated four women seriously over the past decade, but there is no comparison to the siren beneath my tongue. Dessa rakes her fingers through my hair, the slightly sharper points of her nails dragging over my scalp and sending my eyes to the back of my head in ecstasy.

I let her use the grasp on my hair and the arch of her back to guide her nipple into my mouth. Closing my lips around it like a seal, I tease the tip with my tongue and gently pinch it between my teeth. My hand reflexively moves to her other breast, her nipple intentionally between my thumb and finger so I can roll it to the rhythm of her breaths. Her back bows, and she moans beautifully into the otherwise silent room that's painted with history and the scent of her perfume.

Dessa doesn't let go of my hair as my tongue traces a line from her breast down her stomach so I can lay a gentle kiss on the inside of her hip. I'm so close to the small tuft of brown curls at the apex of her thighs that I can smell the sweetness of her arousal, and once I do, I can't hold back. Venturing downward, I settle on my stomach and pull her knees to rest over my shoulders, granting myself the most perfectly close up view of the most beautiful pussy I've ever seen.

"You're perfect, Odessa," I say softly, my mouth barely an inch from her, and my breath tasting her before I do. Her hips move, begging me to stop tormenting her, and my body begs me to stop torturing myself.

"Oh god," she whispers. "Please."

It's all the permission I need as I bring my hand to her and use my fingers to spread her apart beautifully. The flat of my tongue touches her and she almost detonates at the sensation. I can't help but smile as I continue the motion, licking her from the wet heat of her pussy to the tightened bud of her clit. With one whimper from her lips, and the slight tremor in her thighs at my ears, I let my restraint slip.

I only move my mouth away from her for a moment, and with one smooth motion, I slide two fingers gently inside of her. My hips move on the mattress, my cock seeking the friction desperately as her walls hug my fingers in a perfect grip. Just the thought of what she would feel like wrapped around me almost has me exploding before she even touches me. Desperately needing to hear another sound of approval from her perfect lips, my other hand drifts up her writhing body to grasp a handful of her perky breast.

She bows her back again as she pulls my hair to guide me exactly to the spot that I know we both want me to taste. My fingers curl inside of her at the rhythm she's rocking into my face, and I can't stop myself from shamelessly moaning with my lips sealed around her clit.

"Theo, I can't-I'm going to-" she gasps, her sentences making all the sense I need her to make. I understand what this angel needs even if she's too swept up in pleasure to say it.

"I know, sweet girl," I say, my mouth separating from the taste of paradise only long enough to speak. "Let go."

It's only seconds after I speak the command and return to my ministrations that her entire body responds in a resounding cry of release. Refusing to let a single drop go to waste, I drink her climax down like holy communion wine. When she's finished riding the final wave of her orgasm, I slowly pull my fingers from her, unable to help myself from putting them in my mouth to lick them clean.

Before I'm able to plan the next move, Dessa pulls my face to hers, crashing our lips together in a kiss that's emotionally charged and feral all at the same time. Her tongue meets mine, and she tastes herself all over me, but she doesn't hesitate. My length is aching to push inside of her, but I don't rush the tender kiss she's locked us in. As I curl my hips into her sensitive core, she moans, her eyes almost rolling back.

Pulling back from our kiss, I stare into her eyes and brush her chestnut curls from her face. The pace of her breathing is heavy in anticipation and need, but what captures me and chains me to this frozen moment is the look in her gaze. Even in the dimmest light, those hazel eyes strip me bare of all of my defenses and welcome me home into her heart. This isn't just a casual intimate exchange. I can't explain it, or maybe I'm afraid to, but this feels like more. This feels like a significant memory we've yet to make - something we'll remember long past the morning.

Before I can ask her if she's sure, Dessa tilts her hips to line me up with her entrance and nods her head. Without breaking eye contact,

I move, slowly sheathing myself to the hilt in one movement. We breathe together, both adjusting to the way we feel connected to each other in the most primal way. I lay still, wrapped in her and around her at the same time, like my entire being is trying to etch everything to memory. When I feel her pulse around me though, all distractions fade away and all I can think about is making her come undone again.

Pumping into her, she matches my thrusts with the rotation of her hips, and all intentions to last longer fade away. Instead of an intelligent man, I become a complete and utterly willing servant to her needs, her body, and her desire. Our motions are accompanied by the delectably rhythmic sounds of our bodies coming together, and the cries of sheer pleasure as we both careen toward the cliff of our climaxes.

"I need you," she whimpers into the shell of my ear as she pulls me closer to her until every inch of her body is touching mine.

"Then have me, darling," I tell her, and I mean every single word with my entire soul. "Take all of me."

With the last word I speak, I feel her start to unravel. Sliding my hand down between us, I find her clit and circle it with the amount of pressure I know she needs. My body matches her timing, and with a few more deep thrusts into her heaven, we both erupt without abandon, surrendering to our release. The lights pulse once too as if the house is somehow experiencing an energy surge, and I'm too spent to overthink the possibilities that border logic and the unexplained.

Holding each other through the best feeling aftershocks, I slide her to my side, cradling her into the crook of my arm so she can lay on my chest. I'm sure we intended to make conversation, but in this moment, there's nothing I can say that will sum up the experience we just shared. It was carnal and real, but it was also unlike anything I've ever experienced. It felt like a homecoming, and the feeling of her in my arms naked and sated is surreal. This person next to me is quickly becoming everything to me. I think about that until my breathing levels with hers, and we drift into sleep.

***

The loud sound of the ship crashing through the waves wakes me from what was otherwise the most peaceful sleep I've had in months. Sighing at the realization that the crash only existed in my mind, I reach over for Dessa to curl her back into me, but my hand reaches a cold emptiness where she should be.

Assuming she went to the bathroom, I readjust the pillows for her return as I look around the room in the small bit of moonlight that shines through the window. The desk in front of the window is small, but I can picture her there researching and writing her paper. The hand woven carpet in the middle of the room is homely, but still provides a timeless touch to the space. The furniture is minimal, mostly wooden, and somehow fits Dessa perfectly as if she picked it out herself.

Lost in thought, it suddenly occurs to me that she hasn't returned. Striking me as odd, I sit up on the edge of the bed to pull my pants back on. As I stand to button them, a slight movement outside catches my attention and pulls me to the window. I see the dock, the waves less angry than the ones in my dream, and the large white lighthouse ahead. Walking toward the lighthouse, swaying with each step, is Dessa. Her hair is blowing in the wind, and all she's wearing is a sheer white nightgown.

The way she moves seems peculiar, especially considering my phone says it's just after 3am. We did a shot of whiskey, but she wasn't acting this way earlier. My brows crease as I try to make sense of what I'm seeing, and when she almost trips, I move quickly down the stairs and out of the house toward her.

I jog the short distance to her, and when I reach her side, I'm surprised to find her eyes closed tight. *Sleepwalking.* Before I have time to wonder how she was able to navigate herself even to this point subconsciously, she starts to murmur. At first it's quiet, and I can't quite understand her intended words, but as her eyes move beneath her eyelids, her voice gets louder. Her bare arms extend toward the waves where the dock rests, as if she's trying to wrap her arms around the sea itself in a lover's embrace. Dessa mumbles again, this time with a tone of sorrowful longing, and although her eyes remain shut, a single tear falls down her cheek.

All at once, an eerie sensation washes over me. It feels like we're not alone, but I know we are. There's no other access to Corlucius Island, and with the only boat back on the mainland with her parents, there's no way anyone else could be here. I continue to talk myself out of my anxiety, but Dessa's gasp startles me out of my distraction. She turns her pace from the lighthouse to the dock, taking two steps before her body shakes as if she's hit a wall.

I follow the direction of her outstretched arms, and as my eyes adjust to the darkness that surrounds us, I see it. The shadow. The unmistakable shape of a man standing next to the dock looking directly at us. Like a scarecrow or a marble statue, the man doesn't move. He only stands there staring at us. I can't make out his features, but as I narrow my eyes to try, Dessa gasps.

Turning to her, I lock my grip to her arms to shake her awake when her entire body starts to tremble. Her cries are loud now, but her eyes won't open. With three solid jerks of her body, I call her name to guide her back to this island from whatever dreamland she's trapped in with no escape. At the third mention of her name, her eyes fly open and mine instantly widen at what I see.

Dessa looks at me with eyes open like saucers, brimmed with tears and racked with fear. But the part that strikes me as odd and sends chills through my body is that I don't think I'm looking at Dessa. Her eyes are not her usual hazel pools, they're bright green and filled with so much fearful urgency. She looks at me like we're strangers and lovers all at the same time, and I almost forget there's a man standing on the dock.

Only taking my eyes off of her for a moment, I whip my head to the side to see that the figure is gone. I don't even get the opportunity to breathe a sigh of relief though. Her cold hands snake their way up to my face as I keep my hold on her. Turning to her again, those eyes remind me of someone, but I can't say for sure who. As petrified as I am, I can't shake the sudden feeling that this woman is someone else - someone I know.

"H-Henry," the green-eyed Dessa murmurs as she stares into my soul.

Before I can respond, her eyes roll back and she falls into my arms.

Chapter Eighteen

Odessa

Hugging the warm mug of perfectly fragrant coffee between my palms, I inhale the comforting scent again. After the windy night, the world seems to have calmed with the sunrise. The ivory lace curtains move gently with the breeze of the open window over the sink, and the sound of the surrounding sea makes me close my eyes and open my ears.

"Thanks for the coffee," I say to Theo as he sits down at the small oak table across from me. The way the sunlight shines on him makes him look like a golden god, and if anyone could be canonized for their ability to make love, he would easily become a patron saint of intimacy. Snapping out of the flashbacks of last night before I drool directly into my coffee, I continue to check in. "I'm sure my bed isn't what you're used to at the rental in town. Did you at least sleep alright?"

I'm thrown off by the peculiar look he gives me, and a little nervous that he's going to tell me I snored or worse. His gaze levels me, and my impulsive and anxious grin fades into a straight lipped line of growing concern. As his brows crease, his eyes narrow and scan my features for what I don't know.

"You don't remember, do you?" Theo asks, placing his coffee on the table and crossing his arms across his chest over the tight white t-shirt he's wearing. My initial reaction is to be playful and flirtatious, but I'm stopped by the look on his face. "You don't remember anything at all, Dess?"

"I remember a few things..." I trail off as I stand from my seat and walk over to him. When I reach his side, he's still staring at me, but his look has slightly softened and subtly shifted to one with a hint of intimate interest. Running my fingers through his hair, he leans his head into my chest causing my nipples to visibly pebble through the white nightgown.

"Wait," he says as he rises to stand next to me. His hands grasp mine as he leads me to lean against his chest while he rests his back on the countertop. Tilting my chin up to look into his blue eyes, I wait as instructed. "Darling, last night you were sleepwalking. You were outside at about 3am walking alone with your eyes closed."

"Very funny, Theo. Playing into the whole haunted house thing?" I chuckle while I lace my fingers with his at my sides. My smile waits for his to join, but his expression remains frozen in what I can only describe as unsettlement. "You're serious?"

"I woke up from a nightmare, the same one again. I held my arms out to you to pull you into me, but the sheets were cold. I looked out the window and there you were, Dess. You were just walking through the grass toward the lighthouse."

"I've never been a sleepwalker though," I offer, trying desperately to make sense of what I'm quickly realizing is not a prank or a joke.

"That's not all, and I need you to be the person in the horror movie that believes me when I tell you this, ok?" he asks, waiting for reassurance before I nod impatiently. "I saw someone standing by the dock. A shadow. A figure of a man. And at the same time he appeared, you opened your eyes and looked right at me, but..." he pauses, searching for his words.

"But what? What happened?" I push, my anxious fear clawing its way up my spine as my palms begin to sweat against his.

"You looked at me, but you weren't you, but you were," he attempts to explain. The way my face contorts, he can tell I'm not following. "Your eyes weren't hazel like they are now. They were a bright green. You looked directly into my eyes with the deepest intensity, and you called me by another man's name. You called me Henry."

"Henry?" I repeat. No sooner does the name leave my lips before a door upstairs slams shut and the sound of a woman's short wail echoes through the walls before falling into a heavy dead silence.

We both freeze in place instantly, our bodies unable to process what we know we heard. The odd quiet hangs around us like a fog, and we look at each other with wide eyes attempting to nonverbally communicate what to do next. Our pause seems to stretch on for eternity, neither one of us moving to run even if we want to. It's the first time we can say without a shred of doubt that we heard something that bears no scientific explanation. When no further sounds are heard, he breaks the quiet spell.

"I suppose we're beyond saying it's just the wind, yeah?" Theo whispers only an inch or two from my lips. As the adrenaline starts to wind down, we turn our attention to our close proximity.

"What do we do now? We don't have a boat, Theo. We can't run," I whisper back, the idea of no escape lacing my tone with unease. Sensing the change, he rubs my upper arms as if I'm cold and he's warming me up even though the temperature in the early summer is perfect. Allowing myself to drift closer to his chest for comfort, I rest my head over his heart to let the rhythm of steady beating bring mine to match. "I'll call the ferry to pick us up, and I'll ride back here with Dad."

Picking up the landline, I dial into the sea taxi and request the next ferry time. Knowing we have only 20 minutes until we need to be on the dock, I realize that regardless of my fear, I'm going to have to go upstairs to change my clothes.

"If you'd like me to offer my honest opinion, I would remind us of what Sarah told us. While we wait, we could ask them what they want." Theo suggests carefully, watching me for a reaction.

"Come with me while I change?" I ask, partly because I want him near me and partly because I want his protection against whatever is upstairs in my bedroom.

He gladly obliges and we climb the stairs slowly on our tip toes. When we reach the top of the stairs, he puts his arm out to protectively push me behind him as we walk toward my bedroom. The only sounds made are our own, and from what I can tell, nothing looks out of place or moved. My papers are still on the floor and the sheets are rumbled exactly as we left them. Once we're fully inside my room, he bends down to pick up the clothes we tore from his body last night.

When he's fully dressed, I walk to the small dresser to take a fresh outfit from the top drawer, quickly slipping into a simple navy blue linen dress. I lean down to pick up my leggings from the center of the room, and almost lose my footing as the damn corner of the rug catches me again. Before I can meet the floor with my face though, Theo reaches out to steady me with a firm grip on my arm. As I embarrassingly right my frame, the window comes into focus and my eyes widen.

"Dessa, what is it?" Theo asks when he feels my body lock up. Following my line of sight, his motions echo mine as he sees it too.

On the window behind my desk is a distinct handprint on the glass, it's unmistakable shape in full detail staring back at us. Before we can react, the sound of the ferry's horn slices through the silence, and with one look at each other, we're racing toward the front door and out to the dock.

Chapter Nineteen

Odessa

When the world feels like it's crashing down around me, or closing in too quickly, my parents have always been the steadfast constant that I knew I could rely on. As much as I've been on my own after high school, it was my special blend of comforted independence. Free to fly from the nest, but knowing without fail that I could fly back home whenever I wanted. With parents that are retired and in a state of constant movement, I've learned that home isn't a place - it's the people that make you feel so safe and loved you can unclench your jaw and let your hair down. Up until a few months ago, I thought the only people that felt like my home were my parents, but the recent advancements between Theo and I are showing me that-

"Are you alright, Dess?" Theo asks, shaking me from the mid-melt session my heart was in. I should be scared at how quickly we've fallen into each other's lives and arms, but it feels like I've known him my entire life. I nod and smile as he pulls me into a hug, my arms wrapping around his toned torso like I've done it a million times before. With a small kiss to the top of my head, I look up at him through my glasses.

"Visiting hours start soon," I answer. I know there's no need to explain, but I find myself offering one anyway. The wind must have impacted our cell service on the island, because as we stand on the mainland's dock, our notifications sound like fairy bells in our pockets. "Sounds like you'll have a lot to catch up on while I'm with her."

"Looks like divers found a few things this morning and they'd like me to head over to the museum to see what they have. Sarah is meeting us there," he explains, paraphrasing the messages he's scrolling through. When he looks up from his screen at me, he catches the way I'm watching him. "Although I am disappointed I'll surely miss the girl talk."

"How do you know we have something to talk about?" I tease playfully as he nuzzles his stubble into my neck and holds me tighter. I squirm at the tickle and sensation that sends electric pulses throughout my body all at once. "Ok ok, fine, Theodore. Yes, I'll be talking to my mom about you."

"Tell her I'm dashing," he punctuates with a kiss to the small space under my ear. "I'm educated," he adds with a kiss to my cheek as he holds my face in his hands. "And I'm completely bewitched by her daughter," he finishes with softly touching his lips to my own. We hold there for a moment, and the temptation to deepen the kiss lingers around us, but the bell sound of my phone breaks the charge. When I look down and see my dad's photo on my screen for an incoming call, I turn it to show him.

"Dad's calling. I'll text you when I'm done," I say, as I answer my dad's call. Theo touches his forehead to mine before pulling away to nod in agreement. With a small wave, I watch him walk down the dock and head toward the small maritime museum in the opposite direction I'll be heading. With his hands in his pockets, he looks like an ivy league college professor - well, not like one I've ever seen, but maybe a movie version one.

I check in with Dad as I hop into a waiting minivan cab. Moving here I knew I wouldn't see rideshares as often, but the tried and true local cab that looks like it's been through its fair share of youth sports games is a welcome sight. I love to walk, but wanting to reach Mom and spend as much time with her in her room as possible made me thankful for the ride.

Arriving at the smaller local hospital, I get my neon green visitor's pass at the information desk and stop by the gift shop for the cutest stuffed animal I can find. I don't care how old someone is, when you're visiting them in the hospital, they deserve a cuddly plush gift. With the soft blue whale under my arm, I knock on the door to room #312 before entering. I'm not even two steps into the room before my dad is swooping me into a big hug that lifts me off the ground and makes me feel like I'm six years old all over again.

"Hi Dad," I say, my arms wrapping around him in a hug. He puts me down and steps aside so I can finally see Mom.

I was nervous at first, but as I see her now, she looks a lot better than she did before. Although she's got beeping machines hooked up to her and an IV taped to her arm, Mom actually looks a lot better than she did yesterday. She's sitting upright in the bed with her upper body propped up with the blue pillows every hospital seems to use. Her long honey colored curls appear a little more lively and the color has returned to her cheeks, making her smile beam brighter.

"Sweetheart, I missed you," she says with her arms open in a maternal invitation that pulls me in like a magnet. I sit on her bed and slip right into the hug, the plush blue whale awkwardly and adorably between us. When I push it up into her face, she laughs. "And who is this little friend?"

"Umm," I think quickly, trying my best to meet the quirky spirit my mom always has even at the toughest moments. "Mom, meet Herman," I say through a chuckle as my mom shakes his blue fin in a greeting. No matter how old we get or where we live, we'll never lose the childlike wonder and playfulness that connects us. Before I can create a Herman the Blue Whale voice, my stomach growls loudly, reminding me I've only given it coffee this morning.

"Honey, can you grab something for lunch for us? Seems like Dess and Herman are starving," she says to Dad, and there's no way he could ever deny her a thing. She could ask for a fallen star, and he'd journey to the ends of the earth for her without a single complaint. He looks at her and I can see the visible sense of relief he has with the improvement of her condition.

"Anything for my girls," he answers on the way out with a grin, and it's the strangest thing, but it's almost as if they're not themselves on Corlucius Island. Right now, things seem so...normal. Like a regular Tuesday. It doesn't feel at all like the events in the past 24 hours were real.

"And Herman the Whale!" Mom calls out behind him. When the door shuts, we both giggle as I lay down next to her. Playing with my curls just like she always does, I look up at her over my glasses.

"You sure you're ok, Mom?" I ask, sounding just like the child I feel like in this moment. Seeing her look so frail on the island scared Dad, but it also scared me. She's usually so strong, and to see a cold drain her energy and color like that is frightening. As she answers, I watch her facial expressions carefully, looking for hidden pain masquerading as nonchalant strength.

"I feel so much better today. They said they couldn't nail it down to one thing in particular, especially since it started to clear up quickly, but that it was mostly triggered by the restoration. Irritants to my sinuses and my lungs or something. I'm ok, sweetheart," she reassures me. "The one thing I'm upset about is missing out on meeting Theo."

"Just jumping right into it, huh, Mom?" I laugh as she starts to chuckle next to me. Her laugh turns into a labored cough, so I hand her the small cup of water on the table next to the bed. She takes a sip out of the plastic cup, and then looks at me with an exaggerated wink.

"You're lucky I planned ahead and faked this cold so you two could have the house to yourselves," she says with a knowing smirk. Even though I'm not a teenager anymore, I still blush and get nervous about admitting certain things to my mom.

"He's great. Really great actually. Mom, I don't know how to explain it, but it feels like I've known him my whole life. I know Dad wants me to take it slow, but Theo is different. This isn't like anything I've ever felt," I ramble my way through explaining in one breath, and when I look up at her, she's smiling.

"It's not supposed to make sense, it's just supposed to happen," she says in a simple explanation. "And if you made him your chicken parm last night like you planned, I'm surprised he didn't drag you to the courthouse already." I laugh and nod in return. "That's my girl! So the night was romantic then. Good for you."

"It was mostly romantic," I start, and Mom's brows crease when she looks at me with a dark and curious expression. I open and close my mouth a few times searching for the right way (or any way at all) to tell her about the other things she's missed. "Mom, last night Theo found me sleepwalking outside in the middle of the night."

"What?"

"And not just that, there's been other...creepy things. Shadow figures, doors slamming, handprints on the window, and apparently last night my eyes were green and I called him Henry," I unload.

There's a silence that permeates the sterile hospital air, and for a few moments, all I can hear are the unsynchronized beeps of the various machines in the room. There's a slight shift in her expression and I can't quite figure out what she's thinking, but the lighthearted aura from a minute ago seems to have darkened.

"Mom, what's wrong?" I ask cautiously, sitting up and taking a mental inventory of everything around her. Her heart rate is fine, her breathing is normal, but the look on her face seems uneasy.

"When I was at that house...I thought it was just my fever or dehydration," she says, seemingly lost in the forest of her thoughts. When I touch my hand to hers, she finds her way out and meets my gaze with a building wall of tears in her eyes. I crease my brows at the sight of my mom in this state, but encourage her to continue at her own pace. "I had dreams that I couldn't make sense of after I woke up. There were images here and there, but I was weighed down with the overwhelming feeling of sadness. Like that house was built for broken people and their broken hearts. They were all around us, Dess."

"I believe you, Mom," I offer, as she pulls me back into a hug. "I believe it all."

"There's so much to discover in every inch of that island, just please promise me you'll be careful. Whatever presence that was there didn't seem dangerous at first, but sometimes any emotion in excess can cause chaos. Whatever is there...isn't happy," she says with a solemn tone. "It feels like my grandmother's house all over again. After she passed, I swear I could feel her in that place."

"Did you ever see anything?" I wonder. "Or hear anything?"

"Just once. I heard her call my name as clear as day, but when I turned around there was no one there. I thought I imagined it from being under so much stress - that was until I saw her rocking chair move slightly as if someone had just sat down in it. And I never stepped foot in that house ever again," she confesses. "I was only 15 at the time, but even now, I wouldn't."

"How did I never know about this?" I ask her. When she shrugs, I realize it never came up because it never had a reason to. "Will you go back to Corlucius?"

"Dad and I have the project timeline mapped out. We're going to throw ourselves into the work, then pay to bring on some help to speed through it. After that, we'll sell it and choose our next adventure," she explains. "We considered staying when we first bought it, but after all of this, I think we might not."

"Maybe you'll get lucky and the ghosts will like what you do with the place," I suggest playfully to lighten the mood just as Dad comes back in with a few take out bags.

Sitting on Mom's hospital bed with Chinese food in a take out container with my parents next to me, we decide we're all on the same page with the unexplainable events taking place on Corlucius Island. It's an odd thing to be openly talking about as casual as the weather, but it's our reality at least until we get the property ready for sale. Dad might not be as much of a believer, but he's mostly just lucky he hasn't experienced anything yet.

Maybe there's a reason for that, I think to myself. *Maybe there's something else he's meant to see.*

Chapter Twenty

Theodore

Watching Odessa hop into a taxi van is a relief. With the wind picking back up and the clouds transforming to a grayscale palette, I don't want her walking out here without me. The thought makes me pause. The way I feel about her safety is almost possessive, and utterly foreign to me. Whether we've had the full discussion in detail doesn't alter the fact that this woman feels like my home, my family, and just...mine.

As I walk toward the museum, my inkling about an oncoming storm is confirmed as the hustle and bustle of the downtown area isn't cluttered with hands full of shopping bags, but sandbags instead. It's when I see the first windows being boarded that I stop by McNamara's to talk to the older couple that works behind the counter. Just popping my upper body into the doorway, I catch them moving around the store with a clipboard and purpose in their steps. The sound of the small bell above the door alerts them to my presence.

"Expecting a storm, are we?" I ask, immediately kicking myself for the asinine question. "Sorry, what I mean is, when will it arrive?"

"It may hit us tomorrow. If you're asking if you have time to fly home across the pond, I'd say not likely, son," says the man that handed Dessa my sandwich not too long ago. "It's going to be a real bad one this year. Here, we're getting ready to board up. On the house." He hands me a clear wrapped turkey sandwich and a bottle of water. I'm about to decline when I remember I haven't eaten anything. When I reach into my pocket for my wallet, he shakes his head. "I said on the house, so go ahead and get on your way before it starts."

"Thank you, sir. Stay safe," I respond as I exit. When the door is almost closed behind me, I hear him shout again.

"Tell your girl and her parents to be careful out there on the island, you hear? It's worse for ones that haven't weathered these summer storms."

I call out another thanks and reassure him I'll tell them. Making my way toward the museum eating the turkey sandwich, I'm distracted by the fact that they referred to Odessa as "my girl". Mine. And it reaffirms everything I've been feeling. Just as the clouds darken another deeper shade of gray, I reach the doors of the maritime museum. Checking my phone, the notifications are clear, so I know she's still at the hospital.

As soon as I'm through the doors, there's an older gentleman with a white beard and captain's hat there to greet me. Sitting at a table near the front counter are two kids that look to be in high school, one with his hat on backwards like I used to wear my own, and the other holding a shoe box.

"Thank you for stopping my Mr. Montgomery. You came highly recommended by Sarah Goodman, so we're lucky you happened to still be in town," he says holding his hand out to shake mine. "I'm Stanford, but everyone calls me Stan."

"Theo," I offer, my hand grasping his for a less than firm shake. "And you must be the skilled divers that found something this morning."

"Yes, sometimes these storms kick up more than a few things we can add to our museum. Peter and Cal found something a little more unique than we usually get. Kids, why don't you show Mr. Mont-uh-Theo here what you found," Stan says, motioning for the boys to come forward.

Sitting the box on the desk, Cal lifts the lid and slides it over to me. Inside, wrapped in a wrinkled bandana, is an old compass. I slowly remove it to get a better look and begin the appraisal process, but the moment I hold it in my palm, a shudder courses through me causing me to hold it a little tighter. The boys watch me with a slight amount of boredom, and Stan checks his watch before looking at the windows to catalog the pace of the oncoming storm. I move my stiff frame from left to right, but the compass' needle only trembles and shifts in one direction.

"Looks busted," Peter says when he notices the shaking needle's inaccuracy. "I thought maybe we'd be able to sell it for a PS5 at least. I thought all this old stuff was at least worth that, right?"

"Damn, all that and still no PS5," Cal chimes in, kicking the side of the desk. "Would it be worth something if the stupid thing worked?"

"Boys," Stan says sternly. "Let Theo here do his job. And all the things in this museum were donated. I'm not prepared to pay you anything."

"I will," I chime in impulsively, surprising everyone including myself. "You're right about the damage affecting the value, but what you have here is a compass that is most likely from a British owner somewhere between 1700 and 1800. Why don't we do this, boys. I'll pay you each $1,000 right now which is more than you'd ever see in a private sale. And when I'm finished with it, Stan, I'll donate it to your museum."

"Fuck yeah!" Peter shouts.

"Peter Murphy, Jr.!" Stan says firmly. "Language."

"Sorry," Peter says under his breath while Cal laughs. They both pull out their phones and start texting a mile a minute, which I can only assume is planning to pick up the gaming console they wanted so badly.

I'm sure I could have negotiated for far less, however, something about this compass is off. Something tells me I'm the one that should hold onto it. It's not meant to be in the possession of 2 clumsy high school students.

It's meant to be mine.

"Cashapp us, man," Cal says as they both hold their phones to me. Without hesitation, I tap both screens and gladly spend the $2,000 to own a piece of history that without this storm, would have stayed buried in the sand below the sea forever.

As the boys congratulate themselves and record a video on the way out bragging about their discovery-turned-quick-cash, I realize something - I'm still tightly gripping the compass in my palm. Stan turns to answer the phone and I'm left standing in the museum staring at the small brass compass that cost me a couple thousand dollars. I don't know why, but I needed it. While Stan's phone call gets more involved, I decide to walk around and examine the compass in more detail.

I turn left, right, and then in a complete circle as I pay close attention to the small needle in the center. My eyes narrow at the peculiar way it *chooses* to move. It's the only way I can think to describe its motion or lack thereof. The longer I cradle its brass case in my palm, the more it feels like an extension of me, a part of me that had been violently ripped away and is just beginning to regenerate.

I swivel my body back and forth again to attempt to decipher its unique inner workings, but the quivering of the needle has stopped. My brows crease as I look up to find Stan still on the phone with someone at the front desk. Testing my theory that the compass' true north is inaccurate, I take my phone out of my front pocket and open the compass app. Immediately it springs to life, the ease of it being the love part of my love-hate relationship with technology, and my answer is instantly apparent.

In my left hand, the centuries old compass points toward the "N", but the app moves easily and with purpose. I'm facing both of them forward in front of me, however needles (digital and real) are pointing in different directions. My phone tells me I'm facing east, but the compass in my hands holds steady on a true north. If it's in this condition, I most certainly overpaid, but I'm surprised when I turn and the needle moves.

So it's not stuck, I deduce in my mind. *Interesting.*

Waiting for Stan to finish his phone call so I can ask him a few more questions, I wander and peruse the small museum's offerings. The term museum might give an image of a large building of many floors, mummies, or statues. This small structure humbly boasts two rooms in addition to the lobby. The floors creak when you walk through and it's painted a light sky blue. On the walls are framed photographs in black and white with paintings and postcards filtered throughout. It looks as if I'm walking through a scrapbook. Along the walls, there are glass cases filled with miniature model ships, shipyard signs touched by different degrees of rust, snakelike piles of thickly spun rope, and an assortment of items that have been found by locals and tourists alike.

At first, I'm not pulled in any one direction. I've been to plenty of museums with various degrees of funding and structure. I've spent my life holding pieces of time in my hands and telling the stories of when they were new. Feeling a sudden urge I cannot explain, I pull the compass out from my pocket and find it indicates that north is a small corner of the second room. Glancing over at Stan to see him still pacing with the landline's cord wrapped around his weathered fingers in boredom, I walk into the room to find it's more of a library than a museum. It's an archive.

Placing the compass on the table in the center of the room, I walk along the shelves littered with magazines, books, stacks of yellowed paper, and seashells. It's a quiet space, almost like a mausoleum, each word on the pages here telling the stories of seafarers unable to tell their own. It feels sacred. Reverent. The lights flicker once, then twice, and I know the oncoming storm is to blame, but when I glance at the table at the compass, I can't be too sure.

Walking back to the table to stand over it, its needle slightly quivers and I narrow my eyes at it, unable to decipher if it was a trick of the light. When it does it again, it's accompanied by the sound of a book hitting the floor, the slap of it on the hardwood eliciting an annoyed shush from an unseen someone in the other room. Chills roll up my spine in waves and for a brief moment, I'm wearing cement shoes. I'm frozen to my place on the floor and it's not entirely from fear, but I don't understand it.

Forcing myself to move, I pick up the book to put it away and get out of this space that isn't confined, but feels like it's getting smaller and smaller. I realize suddenly that it's not a book I hold, but a leatherbound journal of some sort. A volume of records with the date scrawled on the cover and spine. 1790-1800. Opening the cover feels like opening a door, and when the air conditioning kicks on, the pages flutter like a flipbook of newspaper articles, ship manifests, and logs and photographs of salvaged artifacts. Everything in the room seems to still with the weight of imminence as I turn another page to read the clipped article sealed in a plastic sleeve.

Tragedy Off Corlucius Coast - British Merchant Vessel Lost to Storm. Most Feared Dead.

As I read the title, the lights flicker again, but this time one of the bulbs flashes brightly once before going out, and a weight settles on me causing the room to blur. I haven't suffered from a panic attack in nearly a decade, but the thought I might pushes my body to move and breathe in the air from anywhere other than this coffin of a room. I close the book, grab the compass off the table, and exit back to the front desk to find Stan waiting there for me.

"Son, it looks like it's going to get a little rough out there. I suppose you should be on your way and come back when it blows over," he says. He sees the book in my hands and tilts his head slightly as if he forgot it existed until this moment. "I'm no library, but honor system works here too. Take that with you if you want to, just bring it back when the storm's over. Might as well have something to keep you busy when the power knocks out."

"Thank you," I offer him, and try to not appear rushed when I leave through the front door.

The moment I'm outside, I can breathe, but after a few short breaths, I realize the sky looks darker. My phone begins to erupt in a series of notifications, and when I pull it from my pocket, I am stunned to find that three hours have passed. I was in that archive for...*hours*? A chill ghosts its way over my limbs, leaving traces of its effect in goosebumps over every inch. Shaking my head to clear my thoughts, I swipe to read the missed messages.

> Dessa: Almost done here with Mom.

> Dessa. …she says hi to you btw

> Dessa: Did you just try to call me? My phone rang, but I missed it. Unknown number.

> Dessa: Still working???

> Dessa: Dad and I are heading back to the house to get ready for the storm. Want to join us? Weather out the storm with me?

> Dessa: Dad's pretty set on getting this done before it starts getting bad. We're leaving now so just let me know when you're done. Be safe, Theo. xo

The book feels heavy in my hands and the compass is a boulder in my pocket. As the wind picks up, I pull the compass out to hold it in my hands for a reason I can't explain other than I must. Placed in my open palm, the needle shivers for a moment as if it's finding its bearings before turning rigid. It says I'm facing north, but I know that's not possible. As the compass feels more and more like mine, I notice that it's not exactly the cardinal directions and stubborn needle that interest me - it's that if I were to stay north and follow it, it would lead me directly to Corlucius Island.

Chapter Twenty-One

Odessa

After seeing the color return to Mom's face, and meeting the nurses who are sure to become her friends long after her discharge, Dad's been on a mission to get the house and lighthouse protected before the big storm. Maybe a little time off of the island was all he needed. The more I stay on Corlucius, I understand the sentiment "like you're on an island". It gives me another layer of complexity to consider as I write my paper. We're alone on the island now, but with social media and wifi, we're not exactly remote. I can't imagine how lonely being a lighthouse keeper would be without a close link to anyone else. Now that we're looking at the genuine possibility of storm damage and losing power, we could find out firsthand exactly what that felt like. A small part of me thinks it's what it would want - whoever or whatever is in that house.

While Dad is boarding up a few windows and clearing his work stations from outside the lighthouse, I find myself exploring the house with a different eye. I don't know what I'm looking for exactly, but

I'd like to find anything that can give me a clue as to what could be the cause of what I've heard and seen. It's a lot easier for me to feel a little more brave to look around like this when the sun is still up and my dad is closeby. No matter how old I get, I can still call my dad to check under the bed for monsters without judgement or question, and knowing that gives me a little more courage than I had last night.

Looking out the kitchen window, I watch him hammer away at the nails of the steps leading up to the lighthouse in the late afternoon sun. Judging from where he is on his to do list that he ran through with me on the boat ride here, I can tell he'll most likely pause in a little while for something to eat since the tasks that come after that will be more time consuming. Opening the door to the refrigerator, I pull out everything I need to make him a sub that he can grab whenever he's ready. With the storm closing in and the weather alerts still causing loud sporadic alarms on our phones, he's not going to take the time to stop and eat a full meal at the table, and neither should I. When I wrap the sub in parchment paper and put it on the top shelf to make it easy to spot, I wipe my hands on the hand towel and start up the stairs.

Humming to myself on the way up the wooden stairs, a sure sign I'm hopelessly smitten with Theo, I pause my steps when I realize my voice isn't the only one. There's a soft female voice faintly carried on the wind, a song that matches mine. The odd thing about it all is that I wasn't humming anything in particular. It wasn't something I know, so how is this echo voice accompanying me if I don't even know the tune. When I stop singing, so does the voice, and I second guess what I've heard. Telling myself Dad must have the radio on outside, I take another step and it's met with the sound of a door creaking open. Gathering my courage, I do something I never thought I could do.

"H-hi. My name is Odessa. I just want to say...d-do you need my help?" I ask barely above a whisper, my voice quivering at the unseen door I'm knocking on, waiting for anyone to open it.

A slight breeze gently whisps through the stairway, and when the ends of my hair sway to it, I can feel my heart jump. Before I allow myself to welcome the unease in that's begging to unnerve me, I take a deep breath and remember the window in the kitchen may still be open. Not knowing when the rain will start, I turn and walk back down the stairs to shut it before Dad sees that I carelessly left it open.

When I reach the kitchen, it seems a lot darker than a few minutes ago. It's an odd sensation, that the world can change so quickly, but when I feel my phone vibrate in my pocket and I see I've missed another call from an unknown number, I'm stopped by the time. From the time I made Dad's lunch until now, it's been two hours. There's still no messages from Theo, and I can't explain where two hours of my life have gone. Struggling to explain it to myself, and finding no solution, I twist the knob on the kitchen sink to run my hands and face in cold water.

Putting my glasses back on, and drying my hands, a flash of light like a mirror's reflection in the sun blinds me for a brief second blinking once, then twice. I look through the window in front of me at the lighthouse and I'm taken by the sight immediately. It almost appears to be a scene from a movie with how familiar it seems to be now. Standing strong and tall is the white weathered lighthouse, its black top almost blending into the dark clouds behind it. It's as if the oncoming storm is intent on swallowing the world into the abyss, and the lighthouse is the only thing standing in its way. From the base of the beacon, the stairs are finished just as Dad wanted, and the door is open, swaying in the wind. It stands like an old warrior, worn from countless battles, riddled with scars, but still rising to fight one last time.

Just as my eyes travel up the lighthouse to the top, I'm blinded a third time by a flash from the light, only this time - I see someone up there. Someone shining the light into my eyes.

"Dad?" I say out loud on impulse, but instead of an answer, the scent of heavy tobacco rolls through the house, clogging my senses. Before I can utter another word, a door upstairs slams shut so forcefully I swear the floor beneath me quivered.

Rushing up the stairs to make sure he's ok, I find that the only door that's closed is my bedroom. I only pause for a brief moment before an overwhelming feeling of urgency travels through my veins, the fight or flight in my blood, and I rush in. I'm not sure what I expected, but my dad isn't in here. No one is in here. It looks like a strong gust of wind pushed its way through the room as the photo copies from the library, pieces of news articles, and the carpet in the middle of the floor have been shifted from their rightful places.

Picking up the papers and articles , I reorganize them quickly back into piles on the floor. Knowing Theo might be back tonight if the storm isn't here yet makes me want to make sure my room doesn't look like the storm only existed in here. Stepping on the rug to kick the corner flat with my foot, the floorboard beneath it lets out a groaning creak. At the sound of the warped wood under my weight, one of the bulbs in the floor lamp bursts causing a crack. Wanting to run, I remember what I'm supposed to do.

"Are you trying to show me something?" I ask openly. It's above a whisper this time, but fueled entirely by my fear.

Glancing out the window, I see my dad out at the lighthouse, and I turn back to the rug I'm standing on and kick it completely to the side. Bouncing on my feet, I find the culprit and kneel down closer to inspect it. As silly as it may seem or feel, it's just a gut feeling I can't shake. Something, well everything, in me is pulling me to this one tiny spot. Squinting my eyes, I notice it - the small scratches on the top right corner of the wood plank, like it's been pried open more than a few times.

Crawling over to the desk to grab a letter opener from it, it doesn't take me long before I'm prying, pulling, and clawing my way around the weathered plank. It's stubborn, centuries of forgotten memories sunken into the cracks and holding it tight. Like a crazed archeologist on the brink of an unknown tomb, I drag the pointed edge of the silver opener along the perimeter of the plank and when I get to the slightly lifted corner that's been causing the noise that sounds like the aching of time itself, I push as hard as I can.

Although the wind has started to howl in the distance like a wolf's warning, the world goes silent to allow the sound of a splintering wooden pop to take the center stage. I gasp and pause as the edge of the plank shifts upward, freeing itself from the confines of time. I drop the letter opener and tilt my head to see the tiny corner of darkness under where the plank has lifted, a door creaked open to the unknown. I could be crazy and Dad will be furious that I ripped up part of a historical landmark without the proper tools or renovation know-how, but the pull I feel to this small triangle of depth that just breathed its first breath in I don't even know how long - it feels...cathartic in some way.

Feeling the weight of the world rest in the stillness, I sense that something, *or someone*, is waiting. Pulling the plank upward with all my might, the plank detaches with a pop and I'm thrown backward with it from the force. Wincing as I land on my tailbone, it's instantly forgotten when small particles of dust rising from the place beneath the floor catch the last bit of sunlight. It looks like magic. When I crawl back to the opening, I put my hand into the abyss to feel what I think I already knew - there's something I'm meant to find. As my fingers brush an object, I feel a shiver roll through me as my hair moves in the wind although no windows are open.

Opening my hand and reaching farther, I curl my fingers around what - I don't yet know, but it feels like *mine*. When I pull back from the floor, I bring my hand up to the light to see the hidden truth that's been waiting to be found. There's a tattered piece of fabric, the original color lost in time, that's gently folded all four corners in to hold its contents like a blanket over a child. Carefully and delicately, I open each corner of the fabric as the dust hiding in every wrinkle in time falls freely at last. When the final corner is opened like the petals of a rare flower, a stack of folded papers rest neatly in a pile, letters with a thin piece of twine tied around them in an imperfect bow.

I don't pull the bow open as gently as I unwrap the fabric. I almost feel frenzied to discover something I deeply feel I already know. There's no other way to describe it, and with everything that's already happened, I can't fight it with skepticism anymore. As the letters spill to the floor in front of me, I open them one by one, scanning my eyes through the beautiful antique penmanship, the word "love" repeating itself countless times throughout each and every one of them.

There's probably about 30 or so letters here, from someone in love to someone they loved and I can feel it just by holding them in my hands. As I'm opening them all to lay them flat to send a picture to Theo, I freeze when I see the signature on one of them. Two of them. Three of them. All of them. The name echoes in my mind as I read it over and over again.

Henry. Henry. Yours Always, Henry.

Holding the first letter in the pile up to read it in full, I let out a short scream when the candle in the window sparks itself to life. The flame dances before reaching it's fire upward, growing taller than physically possible before returning to an average flame. My instinct is screaming at me to run away before it's too late, before whatever is coming arrives and there's no way out, but I shake my head to quiet the fear as best I can. Some part of me knows I need to see what these letters say.

"I-I found your letters," I say as my heart shakes the bars of its cage beneath my ribs. "I'll help you."

The candle stops flickering completely and remains as still as if it were made of stone, and the room stills with it like something is waiting for me. Bringing the letter up to read it, I jump again when my phone vibrates in my pocket.

Theo: Dess? Are you there?

Me: Theo! I found something here at the house!

Me: image attached

Theo: I'm having trouble opening the pic, but I found something too. I need to come see you. I'm going to get on the next boat I can find.

Me: It's getting bad out. I don't want you to risk It. It's too dangerous!

Theo: Dess, it can't wait. I'm coming.

Reading his last line of text, I know I can't stop him, but as the rain starts pattering on the window, I chill. The flame flickers once to remind me of the letter I'm holding in my hands from Henry, and my eyes are pulled to the top corner of the page where the date lies waiting.

March 30, 1791

CHAPTER TWENTY-TWO

HENRY THOMAS BIRCHAM

MARCH 30, 1791

To the Dearest Miss Eleanor,

I touch pen to parchment in remembrance of this day, for it is the very day the sun did shine more brightly, and the heavens themselves rejoiced. A simple smile from you is a gift I should wish to repay for the remainder of my days.

I have sailed for the entirety of my manhood, and I do not pretend to know a fairer sight than you in all of the wonders of this world. If all poetry and art in this vast land are flowers, then your beauty must be the root from which they bloom.

I humbly inquired what name could be given to such an angel, and you so sweetly replied: Eleanor. That very name, now as sacred as a hymn, I will carry with me as a prayer at sea.

As I return to my duties aboard this ship, I shall linger on the thoughts of your fair beauty and the melody of your voice. I shall return in a few weeks time, and seek the light in your eyes to guide me for they are far brighter than the beacon of your father's lighthouse. As his tower stands proudly against the winds of the Atlantic, I wish to stand proudly next to you again, sweet Eleanor.

If you find my sentiments agreeable to your dear heart, I should like very much to write to you again. There is much about you I wish to learn, and your letters will grant calm to the longing I endure until the next time I may hear the song of your voice.

Until then I am a servant to your wishes and yours in thought,

Henry Thomas Bircham

Chapter Twenty-Three

Henry Thomas Bircham

September 26, 1791

My Darling Nora,

I have awaited this day for so long, and now that it is upon us, it is unearthly. To be granted the pleasure and pride of naming you my wife will be the greatest gift I should ever receive. I could wish for no higher honor than marrying you at the very church I attended all my life. My heart can barely contain the utter excitement I feel to leave port without having to bid you farewell.

When we reach port in four more days, it is then that I'll secure the ferry boat as a humble chariot to sail to you, my dearest angel. If the candle burns in your window, it will signify your willingness to come to me, and I shall wait for you by the dock.

I must admit, my flower, that I have begun to collect things for you on the estate. Do not fluster yourself with bringing many items, for should you need anything, I wish for nothing more than to provide it for you. All I should ever require in this lifetime is your small hand in mine.

Once we return to the mainland, you may board the ship and rest comfortably in the private quarters next to my own until we reach Devonshire where we will be married. There we will begin the life we so beautifully crafted in every letter since the first. My wages have secured us a fine cottage there and I do hope it makes you as happy as you have undoubtedly made me.

I would not pretend to know the distress of leaving part of your dear family behind. I vow to you now and always that you will never be lonely. You will never live another day not knowing the warmth of my embrace or the softness of my kiss. Anything you desire should be yours, my darling, and I shall live and breathe only for you.

I am bound to you, my true north. My Nora. I am eternally yours.

Until the night I may love you without the fear of farewell,

Henry Thomas Bircham

Chapter Twenty-Four

Odessa

I'm devouring these old letters like a romance novel. How could anyone want a book boyfriend when you have a gentleman like Henry writing you love letters about not having to struggle or be lonely for the rest of your life. *Good for Nora*, I think to myself. As my eyes scan each line of Henry's slanted cursive, the weight of knowing settles in my gut, but for the first time, it's not of sadness - it's resolve. This is what a man deeply and utterly in love sounds like, and this is the way a girl should feel when she reads it.

I know with complete certainty at this moment that Marcus never truly loved me, and as much as I thought so, I didn't love him. Not like Henry loves Nora, and it's not like...I feel about Theo. At the first tiny spark of that notion, my entire body electrifies and my lips curl into a wide grin. The way I feel about Theo is...not like anything I've ever felt.

A distant crashing sound outside breaks the spell I'm in, and I stand, still holding Henry's last letter in my hands. Letting it go feels like losing something, and I just found it, so I take it with me as I go back downstairs, then out the door in the kitchen to see how much more work Dad has left before the storm. Passing the small tree on my way, I pause at a faint sound that I can only hear when the leaves on the branches are still between blows of the wind.

Closing my eyes and staying completely still, I hold Henry's letter to my heart and wait for the breeze to rest. As my curls pause their dance in the wind, I hear it again. The sound of a woman desperately trying to hide the noise of her heartbreak and tears. I see no one, but I can hear her crying and I can feel her sadness surround me. Keeping my eyes closed, I gather my courage to do something brave.

"Eleanor?" I whisper into the wind. "...Nora?" I try again, and this time the crying stops. The silence is heavy, as the world waits for the possibilities of what's to come. Trying one more time to approach the expecting unseen, I raise my voice just barely so I know she can hear me, whoever she is. "Whatever it is you want me to see...show me." Unexpectedly, and for reasons I don't understand, a tear falls down my cheek at the sadness that is so palpable.

The moment I finish the word, the sound of cracking wood echoes again through the air and breaks the tether I know I had with something. Before I can question the source of the noise, I hear a string of curse words come from the direction of the lighthouse in my dad's voice, but it sounds unlike him at the same time. With the letter still clutched in my hand, I take one more look at the tree, and narrow my eyes in thought before I quickly rush to the base of the lighthouse.

Reaching Dad's makeshift work area, I'm immediately concerned with the scene I walk into. Dad is flustered and slightly drunk as the dark clouds continue to creep closer like a plague. He's descending the steps of the lighthouse and struggling to carry the tools in his hands. Approaching him, he trips over a hammer on the ground and curses again as he wipes the sweat from his brow with the back of his palm. It takes him longer than it should to notice I'm standing there, but when he does, his expression seems...off. With a labored sigh, he turns and walks back into the lighthouse mumbling something.

"...and that's why he wants to pretend he likes you because he's just like the rest of them," Dad says incoherently as he kicks a screwdriver out of his way. Looking up at the spiral stairs with hiccups and drawn brows, he looks angry and confused. When I follow his gaze upward within this dark tower, I can see a piece of cloth or rope hanging from the railing right where the darkness begins, which I'm guessing is probably the top.

"Dad, what are you rambling about?" I ask with a slight tinge of playfulness to my voice, hoping he'll snap out of this hazed stupor. The storm and Mom are already cause enough for stress, the last thing we need is to add the six pack he's clearly already consumed. Fumbling for his words, he trips on the third stair and almost lands flat on his ass. "I'll get it, just tell me what's going on." I say to him as I start the spiral ascent.

"You shouldn't be giving that boy so much of your attention...and who knows what else," he grumbles, the last bit trailing off as he holds the railing like the world is tilting. I pause for a moment, my fingers tense around Henry's letter in one hand and the railing in the other. Rolling my eyes and sighing at his drunken ignorant rambling, I continue - and so does he. "All he'll do is lie and you'll leave here and-and when he gets bored after he got what he wanted-"

"-Dad, stop," I say a little harder than I intended, but at this point, he's not acting like my dad. "I don't know why you're talking to me like I'm a child or why you're saying any of this! You're just being so damn-" I scream, echoing in the tower, but my voice is cut off as I slip on a wet spot where the water has leaked in from the lantern room.

Everything happens so fast. As my foot slips, I reach out to grab the railing, dropping Henry's letter down the center of the spiral staircase. Had it not been for the small piece of rope tied on the metal railing that was too far from my fingertips, I would have had nothing to grab onto. Catching my footing, I right myself only to look down and see Dad clutching his chest and struggling to breathe.

Rushing back down the stairs as safely and quickly as I can, I reach him in only a minute or two. I put one hand on his back, and the other I hold out in front of me to get his attention to reassure him I'm alright. He's barely able to look anywhere other than my eyes, and the expression in his gaze is one of sheer terror. From his pale face to the cold sweat and tremors, I'm genuinely worried that this doesn't really have anything to do with alcohol. As he struggles to catch his breath, the scent of tobacco wafts through the air around us like a shackle.

"Out-Outside," Dad stutters and I couldn't agree with him more. There is something about this place that feels too heavy, and I'm starting to feel like I can't breathe either. Sitting on the stairs right outside the lighthouse door that is now shut behind us, he pulls me in for an unexpectedly tight hug. He hugs me like he thought he'd never see me again.

"Dad, I'm ok. It's ok. See?" I raise my eyes to his, and he's searching back and forth to make sure I'm telling the truth and that I'm safe. When he starts to breathe slower, I know there's something he wants to tell me. "What the hell happened in there?"

"I-I-I can't, kiddo. It doesn't make any sense...I just keep seeing-dreaming...it's not real, but it feels so real," he answers like he's trying to organize a junk drawer of his thoughts. He opens his mouth again like he's going to speak, but then closes it. I can see the warring thoughts all over his face and in his troubled eyes, so I take the time to offer something that might make him feel sane.

"I've been seeing things too," I admit clearly and his head snaps up to look at me. At first I think I see judgement on his face, but when he nods slightly to continue, I realize maybe it's something else. "And hearing them. At first I thought it was just a shadow or the wind, or whatever else people with ghosts tell themselves so they aren't scared shitless."

We sit in silence just letting the sky get darker and the wind get stronger. There's still more work to do, but it's impossible to move from this place on the stairs. Whatever is happening here is pulling us apart at the seams, and until we learn to talk about it and face it, I don't know what the worst case scenario could be.

"...and the nightmares? Do you have the nightmares, Dess?" Dad asks me, barely above a whisper as if the demons in his dreams can hear him if he says their names too loud. I slowly shake my head, but I return his nod so he knows I'm still listening without an ounce of judgement or disbelief. "The nightmares are the worst things I've ever seen in my life, and just now what I saw in there...that time I wasn't even asleep."

"What is it?" I ask when I see tears break in his eyes. Placing my hand over his trembling ones, I reassure him. "What did you see in there?"

"I saw that letter hit the ground and I looked up and you were-you were there...you were there h-hanging," he says shakily, the rogue tear finding its way down his cheek. "And the dreams of your mother getting worse. You two are my sunshine, kiddo. The only way I've been making it stop is if I go to bed drunk, that's the only time I know I won't dream. I can't-I can't dream this anymore."

"Dad..." I say, watching the strongest man I know crumble into a shaking mess. I wait for words to find me, but all I can do in this moment is hug my dad. He clings to me and we cry while the storm inches closer. I just hope Theo gets to us before it does.

Chapter Twenty-Five

Theodore

If there was a faster way to Corlucius Island, I would find it. The idea that Dessa is there with the discovery of something important, and I'm not there with her feels unsettling and I can't yet place why. Rushing back to my room at the Bed & Breakfast, I grab my bag to throw in minimal toiletries and clothes in the event the storm makes it harder to leave. Placing a hand in my pocket to wrap protectively around the compass, I rush back down to the dock to pay for a boat rental.

It doesn't take me long to jog down, and I'm relieved when I can see a boat or two in the distance waiting for me to jump aboard and find my way to my girl. *My girl.* No matter how nerve-racking this situation may be, the idea that she's mine brings a smirk to my lips and a warmth to my chest. There's a lot more people out here than usual, and everyone is moving with frantic speed. As politely, but as quickly as I can, I push my way through the people to get to the rental boats before the last one is gone.

Staying calm as I make my way to the boats, I can see the ominous darkness looming like an omen - of what, I don't want to know. I can hear the chatter around me.

"-sandbags. How could they run out of sandbags? Makes you wonder what they spend our tax money on, doesn't it?"

"It's just a storm, we have these every year. I don't know why everyone is freaking out. Back in '89, we had a bigger one than this. Whole town's power went out for a week. Those seniors got to miss their exams, remember?"

"Damn tourists always make a big deal out of nothing. You'd think it was the end of the world. Bet they would fall apart over an inch of rain."

"It's an air bnb, babe. If it floods, who gives a shit? Oh wait, we should vlog this, here - hold my phone so we can get this."

"No, I haven't seen her. Sorry, man."

Looking from face to face, I realize there's only a few I truly recognize. There are people in various degrees of panic from taking selfies and pictures of the looming darkness in the sky, all the way to an older man shouting at a stranger for taking the last sandbag. There are dogs barking and a lone raven that caws three times adding to the overall sinking feeling that something feels off.

I'm bumped hard in the leg by someone's stroller, and when I look up, the man pushing it gives me a sorry shrug before he's on his way. In the short distance in front of me, there's a man with blonde hair talking to each person frantically. I pat my pockets remembering 1 don't have any currency, in case that's what he's short on. His actions seem odd, and he hasn't once looked up at the sky like the rest of them. He's more concerned with his phone, but it's not a casual concern by any means.

Almost at the edge of the dock, and a small black and white rental boat less than ten yards away, I pass two people I've seen at McNamara's. Attempting to wave, something stops me cold in my tracks. There's a phone shoved in my face, and the photo on the screen is too familiar. It's one I don't like in the hands of anyone else. The picture is a cropped version of another photo, and in it, Dessa is wearing a simple black dress with a graduation cap in her hands. *My Dessa*.

"Hey man, have you seen my girlfriend? She's missing, and we're all pretty worried," the man holding the phone asks.

Looking up into his eyes, I have no confusion as to who I'm talking to. Marcus. This is the person that made her feel so frightened and unsafe that she flew across the States to hide out with her parents. No one would do that over a petty breakup. This man is dangerous to her, and the more I look at him, the more I'm disgusted that men like that exist in the world. I imagine my sister and my mother being threatened by someone like this, and it makes the stone in my stomach even heavier.

"Can't help you," I say in a clipped tone that I pass off as preoccupied as I look around him toward the boat. Thinking he'd move along, I move to pass him by, but he fists the sleeve of my shirt to hold me steady.

"Hey, can you look a little closer? We just really want to make sure she's ok and bring her home," Marcus pleads, but the glint in his eyes with the black clouds behind him paint a picture of a man dangerously obsessed with someone that doesn't belong to him. His attempt at wounded concern might have been convincing to anyone else, but there's something about the way he looks at the photo of her that makes me want to ensure he never finds her.

"Again, I can't help you," I say with a bit more firmness, shaking my shirt's sleeve from his grasp. Something instantly shifts in his demeanor and the nice guy mask slips.

"Can't or won't?" he asks, narrowing his eyes and straightening his form. We're both about the same height, but he's holding his body to purposely seem as if he could tower over me. I sigh with irritation, and move to pass him again, the black and white boat in my sights as I pray no one gets to it first. "You know her don't you, you sick fuck. You stay the hell away from my girlfriend, you get me, Jack the Ripper?"

"There's other people to bother, why don't you bugger off, kid?" I snap, the secondhand embarrassment of him using the only name he could think of for a "bad guy with an accent" - Jack the Ripper?

"Stay the fuck away from her, asshole. We just had a disagreement, but that's what couples do sometimes. She loves me, and I know she's here because her parents are redoing the lighthouse on their show. I *know* she's here somewhere. I can *fucking* feel it," Marcus seethes with the type of tone that makes me certain I'll do anything it takes to keep him away from her.

"Spoken like a sane man with a solid grasp on reality," I mumble, shoving him out of my way to get to the boat. "Now if you'll excuse me."

"Why are you in such a hurry?" he shouts without a care in the world as to who hears him at this point. It's that precise moment I realize the same time that he does that I've made the worst mistake I could have ever made. It's a minute miscalculation that I know changes everything, and I see the smug look wash over his face like an oozing oil spill.

I open my mouth to respond but it's too late. He looks at the small overnight bag in my hand, then he follows my line of sight behind him to the boat. His sinister expression curls into a smirk of deviant discovery.

He knows.

"So she *is* on the island, then," Marcus sneers as the temperature of the blood pumping through my veins feels like it's heating to a boil. My knuckles whiten around the handle of my bag, and my molars ache with the strength that my jaw is clenched.

If I could run to her at this moment, I would. If I had wings, I would tear through this menacing sky to swoop down and shield her from this pathetic excuse of a man. But for now, I remain still with narrowed eyes on him to attempt to anticipate what his next move may be. Marcus looks around at the people that surround us, completely unaware of the type of man in their midst. Glancing over my shoulder, he leans in too close to me and I can smell the sweat and desperation seeping through his pores under the uneven stubble. Before I get the chance to say a word, he lowers his voice just above a whisper to speak, spitting as he does.

"If you touched her...if you touched what's mine...if she whored herself out for you, I'll have to treat her like the fucking slut she is," he says, and the blood that once burned within me ices over at the words and intention. Meeting his eyes, I truly see the unmasked toxic and insecure man in front of me. "She'll learn how I expect my wife to act...and what happens when you cheat on me."

I can't explain what possessed me so completely that I lost sight of what I was meant to do, but the moment Marcus uttered the last word of his threat, my body chose before I did. I rear back and punch him in the face as hard as I can. The moment my knuckles connect with his cheekbone, he falls to the ground amidst several onlookers who gasp as they look upon the situation in shock. I barely have a second to collect myself and come to the realization that for the first time in my life, I've punched someone, when I'm aggressively hauled backward on both sides.

"Hey, break it up," a low voice says to my side, and I don't even have to turn around to know exactly what trap Marcus set for me to clumsily walk right into.

"Thank you so much, officers. I'm not sure what happened. I was just asking him a question, and he freaked out on me," Marcus says while he stands, rubbing the side of his face that will undoubtedly bruise. *Good.* "You saw that right?"

"Are we going to have a problem with you two?" the other officer asks, facing his attention toward me, but slightly loosening his grip on my upper arm when he realizes I'm not fighting his hold at all. I hold my hands up in surrender, my knuckles red and throbbing, and Marcus does the same, but with protest.

"Officers, no trouble from me. I'm just worried about my girl-friend, and I heard this storm you got coming in is going to be pretty bad. My father will be thankful you both were here to make sure this didn't get ugly," Marcus replies as he straightens his golf polo, and looks at me to send what only I know is a direct message that he's won. "Sorry you have to deal with this. You can imagine how hard it is to be without the person you love. Matter of fact, I'm heading to her now. Is there anything else or can I go? No need to take this further, right?"

"Depends. Are we both saying nothing happened here, and you're going to go your separate ways and head home before the storm hits?" the officer on my other side asks, looking between us both.

"I would feel much safer if you both just made sure he didn't follow me," Marcus adds, and I can't help my eyes from going wide. "Just a misunderstanding, but better safe than sorry, right, man?"

When both officers look at me, and Marcus winks, I know there's nothing I can do at this moment except nod to agree fully knowing he's going to get to her first. He's going to find his way to that island, and there's nothing I can do but wish on all that matters to me in this world that I'm not too far behind him. I don't know what he will or won't try with her, but out on an island is not where they should be.

"Alright son, let's take a walk," the officer suggests in a way we both know isn't quite a suggestion, and everything in me is at war to move in the opposite direction of where I need to go. "We're just going to cool off in the cruiser for a few minutes."

"Be safe on the water, son," the other officer turns to tell Marcus who is paying an older gentleman on the dock for the black and white rental boat that should have been mine. As they turn, Marcus flashes a smile, and gives me a wave that makes me want to punch the other side of his face to match. All I want to do is run to the dock, swim to her, call her, and warn her that he's coming and that he found her, but all I can do is attempt my greatest impression of a nonchalant man until they let me go.

As we reach the cruiser parked at the end of the street near the perimeter of the pier, the storm's edges finally reach us, and shroud the world in a darkness I can feel deep in my marrow. It's almost as if someone flipped a lightswitch that turned late evening drastically to midnight. The wind howls in response like monsters rejoicing their return in the dark. A few people scream at the thunder that cracks through the clouds, reminding us to be afraid of it.

An officer opens the car door of the cruiser for me, but before I dip my head to sit in the back, I look back out to the dock. Squinting my eyes, I see it. The small black and white boat in the water, Marcus aboard, on its way to the one woman I've ever loved in my life, and all I can do is hope I get there fast enough.

CHAPTER TWENTY-SIX

ODESSA

The storm arrived like the entrance of a chaotic god. Winding tendrils of darkness transformed into a blanket that covered the evening in midnight blindness as howling winds threatened to rip the world apart. Sirens sounded in the distance from the mainland, but I could barely hear them over the sound of the swelling waves crashing with all of their might into the unforgiving rocks surrounding the island.

We never got the chance to board the windows of the keeper's house, but at least we were able to get all of Dad's tools back into storage before there was any damage. We would have been able to move a bit faster, but with him still nursing what will quickly become a hangover, and both of us finally acknowledging the unexplained occurrences on the island, we did our best. Securing the last few things, Dad and I meet back in front of the steps of the lighthouse.

"We need to get back inside the house," he shouts over the sounds of nature raging against the bars of its enclosure. His eyes look tired, and I can barely see the light in them with the storm almost completely above us. My brunette curls whip around as the sky opens up and the unforgiving rain begins moderate at first, but only lasts seconds before escalating to a downpour.

"Let's go!" I shout back, thankful for the kitchen lights I left on to guide us back the short distance to the keeper's house. It almost looks like a blizzard with how little visibility is left only ten minutes after the storm first began to rage.

We start to walk quickly toward the house, Dad grabbing my arm to steady me as the wind almost whips me off of my feet. With the speed and severity of the rain, I can't tell if my glasses are helping me or making my vision worse at this point. Squinting to keep the house in my sights, we both jump as a loud slicing crack of thunder shakes the ground beneath our feet and causes the world to go black. The small light in the kitchen is gone. The lighthouse light is gone. The small safety lights along the corners of the house are gone. Stopping in my tracks, I turn completely in a full circle hoping I can spot the mainland. Nothing - which means there's no power anywhere the storm has touched.

"Come on! We gotta move, Dess! Dessa!" Dad shouts to get my attention, quickly using his phone flashlight to find me and light our path as much as possible. I shake my attention back to him, nodding my head quickly.

I follow him to the house and I'm relieved when we finally get inside through the kitchen door. Everything remains masked in darkness as we throw open drawers looking for flashlights. Something chills me aside from the breeze through my soaked clothes, and in an odd way I can't describe, the utter fear that's coursing through me doesn't only belong to me. It's all around me. I'm breathing it in as it constricts around my ribs like a boa. Panic.

"Shit," Dad says in the quiet house as the storm rages against the walls and windows alike. I turn quickly to him not liking the idea that something worse could be possible right now. "Battery is about to die, so we'll lose this light. Flashlights might still be in a box, so we'll have to use these. Hurry."

Tossing the assorted sizes of candles on the table with a box of matches, his phone screen and light go dark. Feeling around for a match, I find the thickest pillar candle and light it first. The flickering glow of the flame does little to ease whatever feeling that's mercilessly tightening around me. Lighting another candle, I wince as the match burns too close to my fingers causing me to drop it on the table.

Standing the rest of the candles up to light them all in quick succession, I hold the matchbox in my hand, ready to strike when the house goes oddly still. For a brief second, the world stops and I can't hear the rain. All I can feel is something passing through as the candles flicker before the flames rise to 6 inch tall pillars of fire, illuminating only our faces to each other. My mouth opens to scream, but before I can, a bright flash of lightning blinds us and what I see before me chills every cell in my body.

Standing in my dad's place is someone else. A menacing man with a graying beard and thick eyebrows to match. His hat is pulled down almost to his eyes, but those eyes - they shine like silver mirrors in his sockets, and threaten to drown me in their hypnotic look of desperation. An angry scowl is etched into his features, and he wears a body to match with a brawny form that looks like it could wrestle a bear - and win.

When the lightning strike ends, we're plummeted back into darkness save for the candles which have lowered their flames to almost extinguished. It's then that I scream, although it only lasts a second before the thunder follows, sounding again like the roar of an angry diety.

"Dessa! Dess! What?" Dad shouts, his eyes wide as saucers in the dim candlelight. As relieved as I might be momentarily that I can lie to myself about what I saw, there's no escaping what the storm (or this house) will bring.

In that moment, whatever thread was holding the veil together between our world, and the one we can't see, frays and snaps. The world catches back up as if someone pushed the play button, and everything whirrs to life, begging to be heard. Loud crying echoes through the walls as a base melody to the thunder that claps and cracks like cymbals. The sobs that were once hushed and hidden are now wails of unstoppable pure agony. Seconds after it starts, doors begin to slam upstairs repeatedly. It's so loud I don't know how the hinges can handle it. I feel the sounds in my chest like the loud base of concert speakers. I hear a whisper behind me, and turn just as every cupboard door in the kitchen that surrounds us bursts open at the same moment. Another blinding flash of lightning creates a quick strobe light to show us the scene we're in.

The look on Dad's face in the lightning is unlike anything I've ever seen. His fear ages him decades, and for me, I can't tell if the crying is coming from upstairs anymore or if I'm the one screaming through tears. Impulsively, we run out of the house and back into the storm, not knowing which is safer. The sound of a foghorn breaks through the overpowering symphony of chaos and mayhem that surrounds us, but it's quickly lost in the sound of the wind whooshing through the tree, and the waves beating against the shore. Squinting my eyes to where I can hear the sea, I look for signs of a ship, finding nothing but darkness.

Debris circles us like we're in the eye of the storm, throwing a large tree branch through the kitchen window where we had just been standing, extinguishing the small candlelight we had. I'm whipped back and forth between the wind, my body fighting just to walk in a straight line. Every time the lightning burns fast and bright, the island looks different to me - different, but exactly the same, and then different again. The canvas above us wars between indigo and midnight obsidian, and as the lightning flashes, I get a quick glimpse of where the path is.

Standing in between the house and lighthouse, my phone vibrates in my pocket, and I immediately pull it out in hopes that the service has returned and I can call Theo. Using the light on my phone, I run toward the base of the tree for cover, having no desire to ever step foot into that house again. When I reach the tree, I steady myself with one hand and unlock my phone with the other as the thunder roars again. With the one tiniest bar of service, the texts I've been missing roll in in rapid succession and I can't process what I'm seeing fast enough. I have 11 missed calls and texts from Mom, Theo, Savannah, and Ally. As they flood in, one repeated word stands out - Marcus. *No.*

Missed Call from Aly (3)

> **Aly: Dess, babe, where the hell are you?! Pick up the phone. Marcus just posted a story. He's on the way there.**

> **Savannah: Girl, call us back. Marcus told a bunch of ppl you're back together. This is bad.**

Missed Call from Savannah

Missed Call from Unknown Number

Aly: I called your parents. Don't be mad.

Aly: This is serious, babe. Call us back.

Missed Call from Mom (2)

Mom: Honey, Aly just called me. Marcus might show up around town. Please be careful.

Missed Call from Unknown Number

Mom: I can't get a hold of your Dad. Can you both please be careful? This storm looks like it'll be bad.

Mom: Dad says you're home safe. Stay in the house until the storm passes, you two.

Missed Call from Unknown Number (7)

Missed Call from Theo (2)

Theo: I just ran into Marcus. Dess, he knows. He's on his way to Corlucius so please stay in the house, baby. Please. I'm on my way.

Theo: I love you.

Theo: I meant to tell you another way, but it's true. I'll be there soon. Stay safe. I love you.

I almost cry when I see the first few messages come in, but the moment I see Theo's admission of love, I do. Regardless of the storm beating down the world around me, somehow his love shines brightly in my heart. *I love you too,* I think before the rest of the information seeps into my mind. Marcus has found me and is on his way here. Now it makes sense in a way I wished it wouldn't - the sensation of being watched, the missed calls from unknown numbers, the sinking feeling he wasn't going to let me go. I knew I couldn't run forever, and I never planned to, but this time away was supposed to give him space to heal and find someone else to fixate on.

Seeing the small bar of service blink away and my battery icon turn red, I turn off the screen to conserve as much of it as I can. If we're without power and Marcus is on his way here, I'll have no way to call for help if he finds me. Remembering Theo's words, I look back toward the direction I think the house is, and decide to hide when I get there. At least Dad is here so I'm not completely alone. Thinking of him, I turn to notice he's not next to me. No one is.

"Dad!" I call out into the dark. No answer except the cracking sounds of the angry sea and the roaring sky. "DAD!" I try louder. No answer. When the lightning strikes again in a blinding flash, I scan the land as quickly as I can with the second of full visibility it grants me. When the darkness reclaims the world again, I come to the realization that my dad is nowhere in sight and my psycho ex will be here any minute.

Deciding the only thing I can do is hide until the storm subsides or the power comes back on, step away from the tree to walk carefully toward the house. In four strides, I'm back out in the open being pelted heavily by the rain that makes my glasses useless. A feeling pulls at the back of my neck and I break out into a chill. Turning just in time to see what the lightning wishes to show me a glimpse of, I see him. A figure standing on the dock staring directly at me. I can't see the face, but I know who it has to be. Marcus. *He's here.*

Chapter Twenty-Seven

THEODORE

If I dwell on the amount of time I lost also being the amount of time Marcus gained toward Dessa, it will drive me mad. As soon as I convinced the officers it was a misunderstanding, they gave me a stern lecture about decorum and having known better, and let me go as their scanners started buzzing with other calls they needed to answer. It was my saving grace, and the only thing stopping me from trying to make a run for it.

When I finally reached the dock, there was one boat left tied to the metal loops on the posts. It didn't look as big or sturdy as the black and white one Marcus took, but at this point, I'd take a damn paddleboat to get to her before he does. There's no one left on deck for me to pay, so I tell myself when I get back, I owe someone for the rental. Hopefully, the police won't also see me stealing this small ship, but if I want to get to the love of my life, I have no choice because letting him find her is not an option. I did my best to text her and call her from the back of the officers' cruiser, but it kept going to voicemail.

Hopping into the small green boat and untying the ropes as fast as I can, I throw my bag on the deck near the wheel. By the time I start the engine, lightning flashes and everything around me goes dark. There are no more lights along the dock. No lights on the island. No lights anywhere on the mainland. The power is gone as far as I can see. Patting my pockets to make sure it's still there, I feel its form. I reach into my front pocket and pull out the compass as the boat begins to make its way farther out to sea.

When I'm far enough in the water, I realize the dark is an abyss and the storm has swallowed me whole. I hold on as tight as I can to the wheel and open the compass in my other hand. The moment the brass top opens, lightning strikes and the small needle shivers before pointing its true north - directly at the darkened lighthouse. I slide it back into my pocket, and pray to whatever is listening that I make it there.

With every moment that passes, the small boat threatens to crash us into the unforgiving waves. The wind calls to me, and I hear an impossible sound - a faintly distant melody I know I've heard before. I almost know it by heart, but I don't know why. Aside from the howl of the wind and the choppy waves beating against the small boat, I hear a faded foghorn sound once.

Suddenly a chilling sensation slams into me and I understand completely now why I feel like I've been here before - I have, in my dreams. This is exactly how my recurring nightmare begins and ends, and now, I live it. I'm almost thrown overboard as the wind tilts me nearly completely sideways, but instead of terrifying me as it should, I stand still as I begin to hear my dream bleed its way into my reality. The sound of a crew of men permeates the blanketed sound of the tempest, and I quickly glance from side to side just to ensure I'm still truly alone.

Judging by the glimpses of lightning, I'm about halfway between the mainland and Corlucius Island. As the wheel spins faster, I run to hold onto it, and keep the boat on course, the sounds of her song and the frantic crew shouting over the thunder and angry sea ever present. For the first time, I understand that there's a distinct possibility I won't make it to her in time. The idea of Marcus getting near her after he spoke about her like that, it makes me nauseous. Hopelessness and defeat threaten my resolve as every bit of lightning makes the lighthouse seem farther and farther away.

There's only one thing that comes to mind at this moment, and I don't even know if I can do it correctly. *I pray.* I pray that I make it safely to the island. I pray that Marcus saw something to distract him even if only momentarily, and I can slip by him to get to her before he does. I pray selfishly that she loves me too, and that I live long enough to hear those words come from my sweet girl's lips. Turning my head upward, I yell out my prayer. I don't call out to god in the traditional sense, but anyone with perceived authority over the sea. I yell out to Poseidon to spare me, and to the sea itself to carry me to her, but the tempest continues its rampage.

"Please let me get to her before he does. Please let me hold her and tell her I love her. Please! If you're out there help guide me to her! Light the way to Nora! Guide me to Nora!" I shout into the pouring rain and whipping winds as if I'm arguing with an ancient god.

The waves don't let up and neither does the rain. I feel as though I've been on this boat for hours, and the panicked voices of a phantom crew are enough to make me start questioning my own sanity. A small melody plays faintly in my head again, and my front pocket warms almost to a burn. Taking one hand off the wheel, I reach low into my pocket as my fingers close around something I'd forgotten - the compass.

Without any inkling that I'm going the right way, I place the compass on my open palm. Almost instantly the needle points to a true north, and when the lightning flashes again, I realize it's the lighthouse. When the world blackens again, I feel the futility of trying to get to her in time. If only I had the guiding light to pull me to her shores, then I could accelerate this boat as fast as possible. Trying one more time, I call out to the cosmos.

"Send me a sign! Nora, help me find you! Nora!" I yell shamelessly. Suddenly, two things happen at once. The first is that I come to the peculiar realization that I'm not calling out to Dessa. *Why would I say Nora?* I've never met anyone in my life that carries that name. And just as I'm pondering, still scared I might not reach her in time, something beautiful happens - I see a small faint light coming from what I remember as the keeper's house. A small light that pulls me to it as if to say, "let me lead you home", but it's gone just as soon as I see it.

I can't see where I'm going, or if I've turned around. I am no longer able to see the small light I thought would guide me to her. There is a chance Marcus has already gotten to her as every flash of lightning shows I'm the only boat on the water between the mainland and Corlucius Island. When the thunder rolls, echoing through the treacherous sea, I find nothing but the abyss that threatens to devour me.

As the world fades again to black around me, the boat is rocked by a wave that feels and sounds like a truck impact. The sound of splintered wood rings in my ears and I know this small boat will not withstand the rage of the storm. I lose my footing and fall to the slick deck below my feet. Catching onto a small piece of netting before being flung violently overboard, I pull myself to my knees and take a moment to look around me. Surrounded in total darkness and the voices that plague my mind, a tear escapes my defeated eyes, and without anything left to hold it back, I let the hopelessness settle in.

"If you know nothing else in this life, know this, my light - I love you deeply and my love is stronger than this storm. If I should never see you again in this life, I will find you in the next and every other. I love you."

Holding the compass to my chest, I wish once more with every fiber of my being and every ounce of my soul for a miracle.

Give me a way to her. Show me the way to her. Please let me know what it's like to love her every day for the rest of my life.

Chapter Twenty-Eight

Odessa

"DAD!" I scream one more time, hoping that I can warn him about Marcus in time too. Who knows how close that lunatic could be or what he's capable of at this point. I never would have thought he had it in him to cheat on me, but coming all the way out here to reclaim me is unhinged and something I don't want to underestimate. It all takes a backseat though when I see *him*.

As soon as I see the figure on the dock, I run. In record time, I'm back in the house and grabbing every candle from the kitchen table and pocketing the box of matches. The tree branch that shattered the kitchen window is still laying across the kitchen sink amidst the shards of glass and debris. I've never heard the world so loud. From wails of agony and heartache to the screaming of the storm, everything around me is calling out.

Putting my fear aside in favor of making sure Theo finds his way to the island safely, I run upstairs to my bedroom. The doors are all ajar and the crying sounds muffled, like it's in another room or underwater. I don't stop to talk to the unseen this time. Running to the window, to the small candle that's been there since I arrived, I reach into my pocket for the matches in the dark room. Striking the match against the side of the box once, twice, it takes three times for my trembling fingers to spark the flame. Holding it to the wick, the candle lights and I rejoice to myself, but it's short-lived. As soon as the candle springs to life, it's extinguished moments later as if a gust of wind blew it out, but there's no breeze in here and the window is closed.

The slam of a door down the hall makes me jump, and I realize that not only am I fearful of the unexplained activity that's heightened and erupting, but now I know Marcus is here and I don't want to know what his plans are when he finds me. Even if this candle gives away my location, I'd risk it for Theo to be safely on the shore of Corlucius. I'd risk myself for him, and for the chance to tell him everything I want to tell him. Striking the match again, this time with a little more determination, it lights on the first try and I reignite the candle in my window. The flame flickers, then grows unnaturally still and tall before being aggressively extinguished.

"No!" I shout at it, unable to contain the overwhelming frustration and urgency. I don't want to admit this won't work. I don't want to admit defeat. *I can't.* If I stop, there's nothing left for Theo out there, and I refuse to stop fighting for him.

Taking a deep breath, I look at the hole in the floor, the dislodged plank, and letters of love scattered around like leaves in the fall. Clutching the box of matches in my palm, I close my eyes and try something different in the dark.

"If you're here, help me. Show me what to do. Please show me how to help him. Please," I say out loud, my voice quivering as tears stream down my face at the idea that the only thing I have left is pleading to anything or anyone that will listen. "Show me the way."

As the final words leave my trembling lips, the scent of stale tobacco wafts through the room like a heavy fog as my vision blurs. With one hand against the wall near the window, I squeeze my eyes shut, and shake my head to clear the dizzying disorientation as I begin to lose my balance. Sitting on the edge of the desk, I put my head in my hands to try to reset and clear whatever type of panic attack or vertigo this is, but when I open my eyes everything is clearer - it's just not through my eyes.

It's like I'm trapped within an old movie where I know all of the lines by heart, but I've never seen it before. I'm standing in front of the man I recognize from the brief flash I saw of him in the kitchen in place of my father. His beard is streaked with gray and he's angry...he's so angry. And he's screaming at me with a voice that sounds like it could rival the thunder roaring through the obsidian clouds above. He's standing directly in front of me, but only in my mind, although he seems as real as I am. Suddenly, my balance is thrown and I fully lean on the desk as the dizzy spell pulls me under.

"I have done what was necessary! Yes, I extinguished the light! I had no choice in the matter!" his voice booms at me, spittle at the corners of his mouth and the smell of tobacco and whiskey in a cloud around us both. "It is what fathers must do! You have no one to blame but yourself, Nora! I had no choice! You would have left your family!"

"I would have started my own! I have dreams of children and love and-" I start, my voice trembling with the sheer amount of overwhelming heartbreak. With every second and every word, my chest feels as though it's cracked open and my heart's contents are draining out onto the floor.

"-I can't lose you, Nora! You're all I have left of her!" he screams back into my face, and the admission of his consuming grief breaks my heart a little bit more.

"Dear father, you have condemned me to an eternal night because of it! I shall never know the love you've known for the rest of my life! You left him to perish in the darkest depths of the sea with a heart that will break with every swell of the waves, never knowing I waited! You may say I'm all you have left of her, but now I have nothing left of myself! My heart has died, and so too will I never see the light of love! Damn you to the depths right with him, father! You're a damn selfish bastard!" I unleash with every ounce of my being, letting the words work their damage as they were intended. I'm not entirely sure what I hoped for, but it feels freeing to say it. I have nothing left to concern myself with anymore. This is meaningless without love. Everything is. There is nothing ahead of me for everything I've ever loved is in the past.

"Mind your tongue, child," he seethes as he roughly holds my chin in an attempt to remind me of my place, but I don't care. I'm finished here.

"I have no mind left, father. I have nothing left of myself," I mutter through clenched teeth as his hold tightens in a way to keep me with him in any way.

I may understand his grief, for I lost my mother too. She was the sun, the flowers, and birdsong. Without her we have plummeted into darkness in our hearts, and where I found my own sunshine, he could not. I found my own light. I turned on the light. Turn on the light...Odessa, turn on the light. TURN ON THE LIGHT. TURN ON THE LIGHT.

The voice that screamed in my mind wasn't mine, and now I know exactly who it was, and what I have to do. I gasp with a sudden gust of energy, revitalized that there's a way I can help Theo find his way to me. Being out of commission, my parents haven't had a chance to fire it up, but there might be a way. I have to try. Snapping out of it, I shake my head and stand straight up from the desk. As I do, the weight of the past quickly settles on my heart. Henry never made it to Nora...and now I know why. The betrayal tastes worse in my mouth than the lingering scent of tobacco, and my heart burns with it.

Deciding to make a run for the lighthouse, I pull the jacket off my desk chair and zip it up. Checking my phone in my pocket, there's still no service, but the little bit of battery life I have should be enough to help me see inside the top of the lighthouse if I conserve as much as I can. Feeling invigorated with the possibility, I turn to leave the room when a flash of lightning blinds me and illuminates my dad standing in the room right next to the dislodged plank on the floor.

"Jesus, Dad you scared me," I sigh with relief. "Theo is on his way, so I'm heading up to the lighthouse and maybe I can turn it on so he can get here. So we can just-" I pause when I see the look in his eyes. There's a silver glint to them, and he's slightly swaying almost as if he's anticipating which way I'm going to run. Call it survival instinct, call it paranormal intervention, but I slowly reach behind me to grab the paperweight off of my desk. I feel a protective presence surround me, like I'm not the only one in this fight, and I know what will happen before it does.

As the lightning flashes again, I quickly move to the right in an attempt to run around him, but he grabs my jacket to pull me toward him. He smells like an old pipe and alcohol. This isn't my dad, it's *her* father. In this moment, it doesn't matter because I can't let anything stop me from turning on that light.

NOW! I hear the voice in my mind as if it's my own inner thoughts, but I know it's her. Following her lead and saving myself, I bring the paperweight down on my dad's temple and he falls to his hands and knees among the letters of love from lifetimes ago. I don't wait to see how hard I hit him, I just run. I run down the stairs, almost slipping on the last one. I run out of the kitchen past the shattered window and branch. And I run outside as fast as I can to the tall tower that stands as the only connection to Theo.

I lose my footing twice in the puddles that soak the grass from the heaviest rainfall I've ever seen in my life. When I get to the door of the lighthouse, it takes a few tries to fight the wind before I make my way inside. As the heavy door slams behind me, I look up at the spiral staircase, thankful for the small solar emergency lights Dad put in here a week or so ago. Taking a deep breath, I start my climb up the stairs in hurried steps, but careful ones so I don't slip before I make it to the top.

Four spirals upward, I'm almost halfway there when I hear the door slam. I still on the step and slowly look over the railing to the bottom, and the sight chills me to the bone. Two silver eyes in a slightly tilted head on a man that looks like my dad, but isn't at all. He stands there staring up at me as if he didn't even have to look - he just knew where I was. My breath hitches and I'm caught between staying still or making a run for it, and when he moves at an unnatural speed toward the stairs below, my mind is made up for me.

I turn and climb the stairs with as much speed as I can, my legs burning, and my hands clutching the railing tight. Slipping on two steps, I catch myself and keep going as my heart races so fast I can't breathe. The thunder echoes through the dark sky outside, but all I can hear from within this tower are the speed and heaviness of my dad's footsteps behind me getting faster and louder. Fear grips my lungs and I push myself even harder.

When I reach the turn of the stairs where I can see the hatch to the lantern room, I gasp in relief, but my pause is a grave mistake. One second I'm appreciating the sight of the hatch like a sailor who sees land for the first time in months, and then I'm being yanked backward by the hood of my jacket by a force stronger than my dad. I almost lose my footing completely, but I slam into the body behind me. The smell of pipe tobacco invades my nostrils and it's nauseating, but what throws me the most is the menacing expression I can only slightly see. His eyes reflect silver, and his face is twisted into a sinister scowl that conveys sheer inner torment.

"Dad, please," I say through the struggle of pulling myself out of his grip, but it's no use. If I can't use physical strength to pry myself away, I do the only thing I have left - I appeal to my own father. "Please, Dad....he'll die out there." I start to feel his grip loosen, but only slightly. "Dad...Dad...what about Mom? What would Mom think of you? You'll break both of our hearts."

With the mention of her name, he gasps and shakes his head as if he's clearing the fog. He lets go of me, and looks to the rope hanging on the railing next to my hand. Staring at it, his eyes go wide, the silver fading and his blue returning. As he returns to himself, clearly locked into a vision he can't escape, he hyperventilates into a crazed panic. Clutching his chest with one hand, he pushes me back with the other.

"Go, please. I-I can't lose you both. I can't lose you both," he cries, breaking down completely at the visions that torment him that I can't see. A warmth rushes me and it feels like it was meant for me as the words that aren't mine escape my lips.

"If you don't save him, I promise you will," I say, my heart skipping a beat at the finality of it. Dad looks up at me, heartache and remorse eating him from the inside out, and he nods his head.

"Come on, kiddo," he says with a rasp in his voice, still fighting whatever has him in its grip. I decide to keep my guard up, but I don't smell tobacco and I don't see a silver glint in his eyes. He feels like my dad, and at this moment, he's going to do what he's always done - help me.

We safely climb the last few steps together until we reach the hatch at the top. Lifting it and pushing it open, we take the rest of the stairs into the top of the lighthouse. Although we've never been in here yet, I'm praying to the universe that the research he's done will help us. Looking at the prism glass beacon in the center of the lantern room, I can't help but marvel at its design. It's incredible. I want to examine every aspect of this room where few people have stood in hundreds of years.

As Dad fidgets with the engineering of the light, I turn to the windows and look outside desperately hoping I can see Theo's ship. I know Marcus is out there too, but all I can see in my heart is hope for Theo. I squint my eyes trying to find even a small blip of color in the dark, but even through the claps of lightning and thunder, there's nothing. The sooner Dad can get the light going, the better.

"Damn it!" Dad shouts as the sound of metal clanging echoes through the lantern room. Turning to him, I rush over with the light from my phone like I'm a kid again and he's under the hood of the car. "Sorry. I'm sorry. Here, shine it here."

"I thought there would be a lot of switches or a pilot light or something," I say, my inner thoughts finding their way out even in a moment of panic.

"For now, it's just buttons," he says, pressing it once, twice, then smashing it with his palm. "It just hasn't been on in decades...maybe longer."

Continuing to press the button, I jump in and try to with one hand while the other still holds the light. I can see the determination to make it work, but the longer he tries to turn the light on, the more tears well up in both of our eyes. After a few minutes of checking the wires and pressing the buttons in any way we could, the dark weight of defeat gives into a sinking acceptance. As my phone finally dies, we're left in the dark lantern room standing next to what should have been our saving grace.

"Dad..." I say softly, sniffling back tears and putting a hand over his on top of the button. He sniffles and an unearthly gust of wind blows the hatch on the floor closed. I know we're not alone, but I am too heartbroken to be scared anymore. Letting go of everything, the fear, the anger, the betrayal, and the past, I close my eyes and open my heart. I let in the feeling surrounding me, and when I look at my Dad, his eyes shine - one silver and one blue. "...Dad?"

"I...I-I am s-sorry, Eleanor," he struggles to say, fighting whatever is warring inside of him as a tear falls down his cheek. He bows his head in shame and sorrow, and a voice escapes my lips although I know it's not mine.

"...I forgive...forgive you, Father," I say to him as I close my eyes and let the tears fall. I cry for him. I cry for Nora. I cry for Henry. I cry for Theo. I cry for the pain of love lost, and for the things we'll never get to say.

Before another tear can fall, he leaves my hand on his over the button and uses the other to pull me into a hug. The moment I'm wrapped in the comforting grasp of my first hero, something shifts. The whole lantern room shakes violently, and we look at each other confused and scared. In mere seconds, the brightest white light I've ever seen beams through the fractal lens of the beacon, and bathes us in a otherworldly white glow.

Breaking out in a relieved laughter and crying through it, my dad looks exactly like himself in the light. His two blue eyes glow with warmth and love as I jump up and down shouting for joy at the blinding hope piercing through the darkness.

Chapter Twenty-Nine

Theodore

On my knees with the compass to my chest, I waited for acceptance to fully settle in. With no inkling of how close I am to the shore, to the rocks, or to Dessa, I do the only thing I can do - wait. Feeling a tear fall, I hope for her safety. As I squeeze the compass to my chest, I allow my mind to clear except for the way she looked the first time I saw her. She was standing at McNamara's deciding what to order for lunch as her stomach growled, and my initial thought was how she reminded me of Evie from The Mummy.

Smiling with my eyes closed, I travel back to that moment and remember the way her attention on only me made me feel like the sun was shining directly on my face. I can feel the brightness now, and it feels as real as the storm. It's only when I open my eyes that I realize the light I feel on my face is real and coming from Corlucius Lighthouse. I stand up immediately, shouting with sheer joy at the change in course and I steer the wheel west toward the dock. Had the light been even ten minutes later, I could have crashed into the jagged rocks at the shore on the side of the island and met a painful and untimely demise.

As I pass by the rocky edge, what I see shocks me, but I'm not able to feel the pain of empathy. On the dangerous coast, a small black and white boat lay in pieces, with some parts of the stern still floating in the sea. It looks as though it was forcefully thrown at the jagged rocks, and amidst all of the debris, a body lay face down twisted in a way no human could survive. I know who it is before having to look, and I tell myself not to feel guilty at the tinge of relief I feel now that Dessa will never be in danger again.

When I reach the dock, I tie my green boat to the metal loop at the end, and the moment I step onto the wooden pier, I breathe deeply. The idea that I could have gotten here too late, or not at all, is still settling in my bones. All I can think of now is getting to Dessa and holding her in my arms. I'm never going to stop telling her I love her. Leaving my overnight bag on the boat, I pat my front pockets to ensure the compass is still in my possession and when I feel the outline of it, I feel complete. Pulling it out of my pocket, I look at it again as it tells me true north is the Corlucius Lighthouse.

Taking two steps toward it, I pause as the lighthouse light passes over me, it's bright light rotating as it did when it was first commissioned centuries ago. Standing in front of me is the full figure of a man...me? He looks like me, but he's not me. His clothes, from what I can see in the dark, are quite dated, and when he looks at the compass with longing, I understand.

"It's you," I say, knowing. The figure slowly bows his head in greeting and acknowledgement. Something in me feels at peace, but in waiting, and without knowing if it's the right thing, I make an offer. "Come on. Let's go get our girls." I open the compass in my hand and as the beacon circles back to where we're standing, the man slowly dissolves into the air that gently carries his wayward smile last into the wind.

A gentle breeze wraps around me, and I feel the compass spin before settling back to its north - the lighthouse. I know she's in there. I can sense it in the depth of my marrow. Unable to wait one more second without the love of my life in my arms, I break out into a run up the hill and toward the door of the lighthouse. As I get halfway there, the door flings open, and my heart sings when I see her start to run toward me.

The bright beacon circles past us like a spotlight as we make our way to each other and in the light, she's my Dessa, brown curls bouncing as she runs and her glasses making her eyes stand out. She's zipped up in a jacket and running fast to me. But when the light circles past her again, she's someone else. She's wearing a white nightgown with blonde hair and green eyes, and the other part of my heart soars. Back and forth, now to then and then to now, under the light of the Corlucius Lighthouse, the stitches in the threads of fate overlap in a way that defies all logic and reasoning.

When she reaches me, she leaps into my arms, her legs wrapping around my waist as our lips crash together. I hold her so tight, and through our tears, she speaks devotion into my skin as she kisses my cheeks, my lips, my nose.

"I love you. I love you," she breathes into my mouth, and I inhale her admission into my lungs. Kissing her, I feel the weight of the world lift, and it does. The sky calms and the rain slows to a drizzle.

"I love you, my light. My heart's light," I say to her, and she smiles with her entire soul. Before she can respond, there's a whirring sound and the power surges back on, lighting up the house and the sprinkled glow on the mainland. The dock light sparks next and the walkways illuminate.

"Nice to meet you, Theo," her father says as he holds a hand out to me. "Call me Dave."

I shake his hand and he smiles at me, but he beams at Dessa who silently mouths a thank you when she thinks I can't see her. As I put her down, she locks her fingers with mine, and I'm thankful she isn't ready to let go either. I don't think I'll ever like the idea of her letting go.

"You two catch up. I'm going to check the damage in the house," he says to us with a soft smile at her like she's a child again as he walks past the tree toward the keeper's house.

I look into Dessa's eyes and in them find eternity. She stares into mine and all I want to do is tell her I love her until she tires of hearing it no matter how many years it could take. I never want to know what it's like to almost lose her again.

"I love you," I say to her again, holding her face in my hands.

"There's something I want to show you," she replies with a soft kiss to my lips, her fingers laced through mine as she leads the way. "I think I understand it all now."

Chapter Thirty

David

Walking toward the house, I do feel lighter. I don't understand even half of what the hell has been happening, but I know enough to know it's beyond this world, and maybe the point isn't to understand. As I pass the tree, the one Becks fell in love with the second we toured this property, I see something move behind it - or was it someone who looks like...

"Becks?" I wonder out loud. There's no way she got out here and has been here the whole time. As I reason with myself and chock it up to exhaustion, stress, or dehydration, I see her again - not fully, just the edge of her sneaking behind her favorite tree. Jogging to catch up, I call out her name one more time. "Becks!"

She doesn't turn to see me, but I reach the tree only moments later. When I stop under it, the strangest sensation passes over me, and when I look around, everything looks different. It's like I stepped into another time. The tree is still here, the house and the lighthouse are still here, but everything looks...older. I don't know if it's possible to step into a dream while you're awake, or if it's just more likely that at some point I cracked my head on something and I'm still passed out on the floor somewhere.

When the vision clears and I adjust to whatever I'm in right now, I see her. I see her standing there by the tree in the summer sunset. She looks just like my Becca and the way that sends a relief through me, I'll never be able to describe. Seeing her so sick lately has killed me, and here she looks incredible. She looks like an angel on earth, which is how I've always seen her anyway, but here she truly looks it. Unable to help myself, I stride directly up to her and throw my arms around her frame. I feel her hands wrap around my waist and I melt, just like I always have for her. Pulling back to kiss her, I don't hesitate. She's everything to me, and she tastes like my very own heaven.

"I missed you so much, my love. I'm so sorry. I'm sorry," I whisper to her in between the frantic kisses she lets me steal. I don't know what I'm sorry for, but I feel it deep in my soul. I am drowning in the grief and regret that wrap around my ankles and threaten to drag me to the depths. I can barely stand to look at her now, my angel. How could I let her see me? How can she still love me after all I've done? But like the holy soul she is, she raises my chin to meet her gaze.

"You have acted out of heartache, my dear, and now our tree will bear no beauty. Flowers cannot bloom in cursed earth. You must let her go," she whispers in a voice that sounds like the sweetest melody. "Let our daughter go."

"She'll leave us," I cry, but I don't know what I'm saying. It's my life, but it isn't. I don't know what's happening, but I know I'm part of it. My angel touches her lips gently to my forehead in an adoring soft kiss before holding my face in her warm hands. The sunlight behind her looks like a halo, making it even more believable that she is my holy love. Feeling everything but truth melt away, I admit what I've been holding. "If I do, she'll leave me."

"Oh my darling, that is precisely what she is supposed to do - fly," she says softly with a smile that is meant to comfort me through this. I let out an unexpected gasp that starts the cry I've been holding in while she continues. "You mustn't think of it the way you do, dear. Our Nora is the best parts of us - our love. Don't you want to see what our little light creates in this vast world? Children, stories, grandchildren, art..." she trails off like she's in a daydream before continuing, all with the same loving look in my eyes. I don't understand why she's telling me this, but I feel it transform me. "When she flies, we fly with her, my darling. Let her love like we loved. Let her have the most beautiful thing this brave world can offer her. Let her love."

With another kiss to her lips, I feel I don't deserve the peace she's showing me how to find within. If I could stay in this moment, I would live in it with her here just like this with the sun kissing her skin as I kiss her lips, her honey waves glowing golden, and her in my arms making me wish for eternity.

"Now you must see," she says with a look of sadness in her eyes. "Remember her," she whispers as she places her hands on me. One hand on my heart and one over my eyes, the beautiful sun is darkened for a moment and I feel like I'm being pulled through a tunnel.

After the storm, she was different. She still tended to the house, to the grounds, and to me, but the light in her eyes was gone. The tempest had raged, and I along with it. That night, I remember. I'd indulged too much on the whiskey I'd collected, and when I found the stack of letters under her bed, I felt betrayed and angry. After everything I've done for my daughter, to imagine she'd leave it all behind for some rake. I couldn't think of a more insulting action. To think she would leave me without a word.

When she had her night tea, I'd poured in the remedy for sleep the apothecary gave me. It wasn't to hurt her, but to let her sleep. While she slept, the storm raged. I walked the stairs up up up to the top of the lighthouse, and in the lantern room...I committed to it. I extinguished the light. I protected her by keeping her from making the worst mistake of her life. I did the right thing. I didn't know the ship would crash against the rocks. I didn't mean for anyone to get hurt.

Nora mourned the loss of the ship and of her love, and I kept my secrets like a good father. One day I knew she'd find a nice young man and settle down on the mainland. I knew it would only take a while for her to mourn. It would be worth it to save her from a mistake as critical as this. Over the weeks after the news of the wreck and lives lost, she still mourned. She never smiled. She never sang the song her mother taught her. She never looked at me.

It was the night she found out my secret about the light that changed everything. I'd had too much to drink, and a simple slip of the tongue ruined everything.

"I have done what was necessary! Yes, I extinguished the light! I had no choice in the matter!" I shouted at her, still drunk, but trying to remain coherent. "It is what fathers must do! You have no one to blame but yourself, Nora! I had no choice! You would have left your family!"

"I would have started my own! I have dreams of children and love and-" she starts, but I refuse to let her turn this against me.

"-I can't lose you, Nora! You're all I have left of her!" I screamed at her, my heart breaking at the reminder that the only woman I've ever fallen in love is gone and won't be there to sing to me when we're old like she promised.

"Dear father, you have condemned me to an eternal night because of it! I shall never know the love you've known for the rest of my life! You

left him to perish in the darkest depths of the sea with a heart that will break with every swell of the waves, never knowing I waited! You may say I'm all you have left of her, but now I have nothing left of myself! My heart has died and so too will I never see the light of love! Damn you to the depths right with him, father! You're a damn selfish bastard!" Nora unleashes at me, and although on some level, I know I deserve it, I'm so angry.

"Mind your tongue, child," I sneered at her while I grabbed her face. I wanted her to know how hard it's been to hold this secret inside just to keep our family together.

"I have no mind left, father. I have nothing left of myself," she said and it undoes me. When I look into her green eyes, she's right. Where there used to be the color of green grass after a healthy rain, all that remains is a dull shade of what it used to be. "Now if you'll pardon me, I'm not feeling well. I'm off to bed."

I let her go and she blankly walked up the stairs to her room. The door shut softer than a whisper, and in the morning it still remained in place. I offered her a meal in the afternoon, and she refused. I took a trip to the mainland for supplies, and when I returned, the door was still shut.

When night finally fell, I'd let myself indulge in the new bottle I'd purchased at the general store. As darkness settled on the world, I set off to turn the light on. Holding my lantern, I walked past the tree where underneath my wife was buried and gave her a nod - something I always did to imagine she was still with me, sitting under the tree reading to me from her favorite book.

When I got to the lighthouse door, I was surprised to find it unlocked and ajar. It was dark inside, every lantern extinguished and black as midnight. I walked in and let the door shut behind me, but when the wind blew, dozens of papers fluttered all around my feet. Leaning down,

I picked up one...then two...and I knew what they were. Every letter Henry had written to Nora. Every one filled with love and devotion and plans for a beautiful future in the English countryside. It was nothing that I'd thought, but it was still a life away from here.

Hearing a noise, I look up to find the lanterns at the top of the stairs were still lit and I squint my eyes to see what's moving up there. When I realize what I'm seeing, I scream. I can't stop screaming. I screamed until the back of my throat was raw and my voice had gone. I'd seen her bare feet first, swaying in the center of the spiral staircase like she was floating. In my drunken stupor it had taken a bit longer for me to understand that my daughter wasn't floating...she was hanging. My beautiful girl with the green eyes. My daughter. My Nora. My light.

Something happened to me that night. Something died in my heart when my Nora died in that lighthouse. It took hours to bring myself to cut her down and carefully let her back to the ground. I carried her to her mother's place under the tree, and buried her there so they could stay together. Maybe there she could find the solace she wasn't able to find with me.

When I went into town, the shopkeepers continued to ask about her. I couldn't bring myself to watch her die over and over every time I had to tell it. I couldn't mourn her, so I gave her the only thing I had left - stories. With every venture to the mainland, I filled their heads with stories of what she wanted. I told tales of her husband, their children, her art, and her love of singing. I told fanciful stories of their lives in England and I let her live her life to the fullest.

In the end, I had no one. My last thoughts were of my wife and daughter, both, and how I wished they'd buried me instead.

I gasp for air, and turn to place my hand on the tree as I dry heave and cough. Everything I've just seen in my mind could tear even the most sane person to pieces. The heavenly image of Becca, or the woman who looks like her, is gone and I'm back in the dark under the tree she loves.

Falling to my knees, I let out a sob that ripples through my entire body, tearing through every part of me. Without putting any thought behind it, I begin to claw at the ground as my nose runs and tears blur my vision. I rip up grass, and claw my through the mud made from the storm that's lifting. I dig with my bare hands until my nails are so full of dirt that they burn at the intrusion, but I don't cease. I can't stop. Breaking out into a sweat, I don't realize that I'm knee deep in muck.

Wiping my brow, I return to my task, my fingers sore and my upper body burning from the movement. I don't know how long I've been digging, but I know I'm finished when my nails scrape something hard. Sitting back on my heels, I know. Even in the darkness, I feel it, and as the beacon circles past us, the pit is bright for only a second. In that moment of white light, I see a curse and the opportunity for salvation.

CHAPTER THIRTY-ONE

ODESSA

Sitting on the floor of my bedroom with Theo, he sorts through the letters while I hold the compass. It feels familiar and significant, but so does sitting cross legged on the floor with him. The house seems lighter, the world seems softer, and with the power back on, it's a lot less scary. Right now, it just looks like a house, and we just look like a new couple bonding over a common interest.

"So then he never made it to her," he says as we put the jumbled pieces of history's puzzle together. "They never ran away together."

"I guess they weren't as lucky," I answer, stars still in my eyes when I look at him with his dark hair still wet from the rain and swept back. He smiles back at me as he tucks one of my curls behind my ear, leaving his hand on the side of my jaw to gently pull me into his lips.

I melt into his hold, every muscle in my body liquifying at his touch, and kiss him like I almost lost him. He returns the fervor, our tongues and lips locked into a display of passion I can feel everywhere. Slightly moaning into his mouth as I rake my fingers through his hair, tugging at the roots like he likes, he suddenly breaks the contact.

"Dess, wait," he says, then groans at how painfully difficult it is to stop touching each other. With a steady hand, he holds my face and I open my eyes, seeing the seriousness in his gaze. "Baby, I have to tell you something, ok?"

I sit back and wait, my body going still and after everything we've been through, I'm not sure anything could scare me as much as losing him. But still I wait for him to tell me. He takes both of my hands in his, and takes a deep breath.

"Marcus got to the island," he starts. A chill goes down my spine at the thought of him lurking somewhere on the property, but Theo squeezes my hands and shakes his head. "There was no light. He got close, but his boat was destroyed on the rocks. He's...he's dead down there, Dess."

At first I laughed out of shock. I'm not sure what else to do, and my body chose for me. Throwing my hand over my mouth, I gasp. Theo rubs my back, carefully watching my reaction, ready to console me at a moment's notice, but that's the problem.

"I'm a terrible person," I whisper through the fingers over my lips. Pulling my hand away, he creases his brow in concern. "I feel...re-lieved." I admit quietly, wincing at the judgement that could follow.

"No, baby, come here," he reassures me and pulls me into his lap, wrapping his arms around me. Rubbing my back and placing a gentle hand on the back of my head, he rocks us softly in comfort. "You're not a terrible person. You're safe now, and it's ok to be relieved. It's ok."

I wrap my arms around his neck and hold on, nuzzling my nose into the small space between his neck and his ear where he smells of sea salt and wind. He kisses my hair, and pulls us both to a stand.

"I'm going to call the police so they can come and handle it," he says, pulling his phone out of his pocket. "You should plug yours in and text your friends so they know you're safe, baby."

I nod to him, thankful he's here to help handle this part of it. I don't want anything to do with Marcus, and I don't want to see the body. I just want to pretend he never existed. As Theo kisses my head again, he moves to the hallway to call the police, and I plug my phone into the charger next to the bed. The moment I do, it lights up and before I read any messages, I text Aly and Savannah in a group chat.

> Me: Hey, I'm ok and the storm is over.

> Aly: Did you see Marcus????

> Savannah: Want me to come kick his sorry ass?

> Me: He was in a boating accident here. He tried to get to the island during the storm, and his boat wrecked.

> Aly: Well when he's out of a cast, we can put him back in one

> Me: He didn't make it

> Savannah: He's fucking DEAD?!!!

> Me: I'm just telling you before you see it anywhere, but I have to go. Theo called the police and they're on the way to the island.

Savannah: Ohhhhhh Theooooo called themmmmm

Aly: Babygirl, don't start. Let her deal w one thing at time.

Savannah: Ugh ok fine, but details when you come home

Me: Deal. Gotta go. Love you

Aly: ily

Savannah: me tooooo

"Ok, they'll be here within the hour. Turns out they didn't get as much damage as they thought they would, just a lot of flooding," Theo says as he comes back into the room.

"Does Dad know about Marcus?" I ask as he snakes a hand around my waist. Shaking his head, we both look toward the window to see where he went. "We should go tell him before the police get here."

"Ok, but hey," he says, turning me toward him. When my eyes meet his, I'm putty again, and the smirk on his face tells me he knows it too. "Don't forget I love you."

"I love you too," I return with a smile, letting him steal one more kiss before we walk back downstairs, hand in hand.

When we don't see Dad in the kitchen, we walk back outside to look for him. The scene outside is beautiful as the earliest part of dawn begins to break, giving the world a warm glow. Theo holds my hand as we stand on the grass looking back and forth for Dad. Glancing over at the tree Mom loves, I squint to see him.

"What is he doing?" I say out loud as I watch in confusion. "Is he digging a grave?"

"He wouldn't bury a body for you would he?" Theo asks, and before we can both laugh, we exchange glances and make a run for it. We know how much my dad loves me, and would he be the type of parent to genuinely bury a body? Absolutely he would. "Shit."

Running over to where Dad is already knee deep in what definitely looks to be a grave, we stop when we see the state he's in. Tears streaked face with smudges of mud, he looks frenzied.

"Dad, you can't, ok?" I say to him with my palms out to reassure him I'm not a threat just in case he isn't quite himself. "The police are on their way. You have to let them deal with him. Please, Dad."

Looking up at me from the grave he's clawed through, I freeze when I see that peeking out of the mud are bones. We exchange glances with Theo as we're all forced to face what he's uncovered.

"Marcus is dead," Theo says, his tone steady. Dad nods, and carefully bends down to pick up the bones. I can't explain it, but as he touches the bones to lift them, my head spins and I can't feel my legs.

"I can't see," I mutter before I feel myself begin to faint. The last thing I feel is Theo catching me to guide me slowly to the ground.

Flashes and images whiz by me in my mind like walking through the projector room of an old theater. I can see pieces in motion of several different things at different moments, but the emotions they carry hit me all in unison. A stolen glance in the general store from the most handsome man they had ever seen. A mother sick in bed, holding onto life as it slips away like fine sand in an hourglass. A hidden letter filled with pressed flowers and ribbons. A family dinner of three, then two. A heart's flutter at the finger touch when letters are exchanged. A smile to melt the ice. A plan for forever in love. A storm. A shipwreck. A lover lost in the tide. A lover lost by their own hand. A lie. A story. A secret.

Sitting up as quickly as I can, I hold the front of my head to combat the spins that follow. Knowing every piece of the puzzle now, I cough, trying not to let the nausea take me under. When I look up, Dad and Theo are standing over me with a hand out. Placing a hand in each of theirs, I let them pull me up to my feet. Looking at the blanket on the ground, I know exactly who is in there.

"It's Eleanor," Dad says, and when Theo doesn't react, I know everyone knows the truth. The secrets of the past are revealed as the sun rises a little higher in the sky, bringing with it an aura of new hope and a fresh start. "We'll give her to the police."

"No," I say quickly and both men turn to me with matching raised brows. "We give her to the sea. We give her back to him. To Henry."

As soon as the words leave my lips, they both nod, knowing it's exactly what Nora and Henry would have wanted. To wait centuries never being close enough to each other, they deserve to finally rest together. It's what I would want if it were me. Dad picks up the blanket that contains what time has left of Eleanor, and we walk to the edge of the dock - the exact place the dark figure always stands, and it dawns on me that's exactly who it was because he was unable to come any closer.

"Should we say something first?" Theo asks as Dad kneels with her bones toward the sea. I slip my hand into Theo's, a tear falling down my cheek, before I start. "We have her letters in there with her, Dess."

"Not everyone knows what it feels like to fall in love. As short as Eleanor's life my have been, and as heartbroken as she was, there was a brief moment where her light was the brightest shine. I hope you dance with Henry every single day, Nora. I hope he loves you through eternity," I say softly as I nod to Dad. He lays the blanket carefully on top of the water's surface and as it begins to sink, Theo places the compass with it.

When the blanket and compass are completely submerged, a moment of silence passes by us and we let it. Dad puts an arm around my shoulder and Theo squeezes my hand as the secrets of the past are finally laid to rest. As the water oddly stills for a minute or two, the breeze picks up, circling around us as we stand in the glow of the sunrise of a brand new day.

CHAPTER THIRTY-TWO

ODESSA

With the officers came the coroners. While the coroners handled Marcus' body on the rocks, I sat at the kitchen table with Officer Sahagun and Officer Pingleton. They both had their small notebooks out, taking down a few words here and there for later reference. Theo and Dad stayed outside near the window where they'd worked to pull the branch out of.

"Then as soon as the lighthouse light came on, we could see everything, plus the power coming back on really helped so we could call you. I didn't see Marcus at all. My, umm, Theo is the one who first saw the wreckage as he docked," I ramble to sum up the story I gave them. I left out the part about ghosts because honestly, of course I would.

"I'm sorry, can we go back to your statement quickly?" Officer Sahagun looks at me with her brows creased into a confused expression. "You're stating the beacon at the top of that lighthouse was on?"

"Well, yeah, Dad and I went up there since it was so dark, and I wanted to make sure Theo could see his way here," I explain, unsure of the point.

"Ma'am, that light hasn't been on in decades. I doubt it even works," she says, and I stand from the table to prove a point. Walking to the broken window, I stare over at the Corlucius Lighthouse...it's dark in the lantern room. There is no light. "And we never lost power on the mainland, but if you did here that would still make sense. Sometimes those things can get a little spotty."

"But then how do you explain why Marcus crashed?" I ask, curiosity piqued and filling my head with questions.

"Early reports are coming in of someone matching his description. Intoxicated. His accident may have been under the influence," Officer Pingleton adds as he sips the glass of Diet Coke he asked for. "It's another reason why we wanted to talk to you. We understand you and your parents have a restraining order, so his very presence here was unlawful and in violation of a court order. He was also wanted on a bench warrant for missing a court date with his most recent assault and harassment charges. We wanted to ensure you were safe out here. You are on an island after all."

"Oh right, the storm."

"That too, but we were thinking more about Marcus. We found a few things in the wreckage that he must have had on his person, and let's just say it's a relief that he did not come into contact with you directly," Officer Sahagun adds while Officer Pingleton gives her a side eye that she sees, but disregards. I crease my brows in confusion, and she elaborates, but very quietly. "We're not able to disclose the particular items because it is an active crime scene and investigation, however I will say, it laid out what appears to be clear intent for malicious bodily harm."

"Then I'm glad he never made it past the shore," I say as I rub my upper arms to comfort myself at the chill that runs through me when I think of what I will never know Marcus could have been capable of. "I'm sorry if that's cruel to say."

"Understandable, ma'am. I have a daughter about your age too. We'll let you know if we need anything else. Until then, we'll be out here for a bit longer clearing the wreckage, but you're free to come and go," Officer Pingleton responds and they both put their small memo pads back into their front pockets. Standing from the table, they give me a nod and walk out the door toward the place on the rocks where the coroner is still working on zipping up one black bag.

As they exit, Dad passes them with a matching nod. He walks into the kitchen with his phone pinched between his shoulder and his ear wearing a look on his face of giddy excitement. Theo is not far behind him, his entire face lighting up the moment he sees me, and I warm at the way I affect him.

"Ok, I'll tell them...mm hmm...ok, honey, we'll be there," Dad says in conversation. When he ends the call, he connects his phone to the charger on the counter and motions toward the mainland. "Your mother says we have two hours to get there and pick her up because she made reservations at a place for brunch."

"You can take the girl out of California, but not California out of the girl. She knows they don't have avocado toast, right?" I laugh, and Dad chuckles. Theo joins in and we both look at him with a smile.

"I don't know why you're laughing, kid. She's about to make this whole brunch about you two, and your entire future plans," Dad shrugs, knowing his wife better than anyone. I know he's right too. She's hated being so far removed from us, but I'm glad being on the mainland kept her safe.

"The future is all I see when I look at her," Theo says with a look of adoration in my direction, and my eyes go wide. It's not that I haven't thought about it, it's just that being with Marcus for years where even the whisper of taking the next step would launch a fight conditioned me to expect negativity around it.

"I know the feeling," Dad says as he twirls his wedding ring on his finger with a smile that looks like he's trapped in the happiest memory. "If you find it, never let her go."

"I don't plan on it," Theo responds with a hand on my shoulder, and the tears in my eyes collect at the corners, threatening to plummet. I put my hand over his, and smile with a blush. When Dad makes eye contact with me, he returns the soft grin, and we share a nonverbal moment of understanding that seems to say *everything is ok and I'm happy for you*.

***

Setting foot on the mainland after everything that's happened feels surreal. The late morning sun is shining and people are out and about like the events in the past 24 hours never happened. Some of them whisper in our direction, the talk of Marcus having already reached the masses of this small coastal town, but for the most part, it's quiet. A few shop owners are sweeping the leaves and debris the wind cluttered at their doorsteps, and they tilt their head in acknowledgement as we walk by.

We hop in the minivan cab to the hospital, Theo's hand never leaving mine as we share the bench seat together in the back. His thumb traces lazy circles on the back of my hand as I rest my head on his shoulder. Being with him feels so comfortable, like every movement we make has been already made countless times throughout eternity.

The moment we get to the hospital, I can feel Dad's anticipation to see her. With the way he's fidgeting, you'd think he was going on a first date with the prom queen. We stop in front of the hospital and my Dad's face falls.

"What's wrong?" I ask quickly, sensing the shift.

"I don't have any flowers," he says with open palms like he has nothing to offer a queen in need of devotion.

"We'll take care of the flowers," Theo offers and Dad looks at him with a saving smile. "You go get your girl."

"Yup, you can stay," Dad jokes, although I already knew he liked Theo a lot. This time, Theo knows it too, and he smiles even wider when Dad pulls him in for a hug complete with a back pat.

Watching my Dad run into the hospital like he's about to do an airport scene in a cheesy rom-com, I smile. Theo laces his fingers through mine and we turn to walk a little farther down the street where the florist is already setting up the day's selections outside. The air smells of the freshly fallen rain mixed with the breeze off of the sea, and if I could melt it into a candle, I'd burn it every day to remind me of this moment.

Before we walk into the flower shop, we take a small detour to the water's edge to watch the sun reflect off of the waves. The island is in the distance, but it looks so much smaller. Standing in front of him, he wraps his arms around my waist and kisses the top of my head. We stand there in silence, letting the world hold us in this space like lovers.

"Theo?" I say softly, not wanting to break the peace, but unable to hold my thoughts to myself anymore. He hums in response, and I know I have his attention. "Was that...us? What I mean is what if...I mean...do you think reincarnation is possible?" Instantly feeling like

I should have shut up because Marcus hated my endless questions, Theo turns me around in his arms to face him with a gentle loving in his eyes.

"I haven't a clue. There are things that defy all religious texts and scientific methods alike, things beyond our human comprehension, but above it all, there's only one thing I can deduce with absolute certainty, and it's that if it's real, it must only mean that I'm destined to love you in every lifetime," he says without wavering. Looking into my eyes, he brings his hands to the sides of my face and touches our foreheads together as the sun shines between us. "My Odessa, my soul's odyssey toward the light. I have always searched for you, and I am nothing if but lucky to have found you in this life where I can hold you and tell you this."

"Theo-" I start, a tear escaping down my cheek, but he continues as his thumb wipes it away.

"-Whether I am Henry or Theodore or countless other names, the only label I want to carry is yours. Tell me I'm yours, Dessa. Tell me this eternal torment of separation in other lifetimes can end and I can belong to you, body and soul, and go wherever you are," he says, his mouth so close to mine I can feel the warmth of his exhale on my lips.

"No ocean, or darkness, or storm can separate us, Theo. I love you," I whisper and push forward the mall space to press my lips to his in a soft kiss. "I love you," I tell him again with a matching kiss that he returns. "I want to give you everything and never go a day without you."

"I don't know how we've lasted so long without this," Theo says and kisses me deeper.

"Painfully," I add with a smile, only half joking.

"That ends now - for us, and all versions of us," he declares, and it carries the weight of everything we've gone through as Nora and

Henry, or as us. Kissing him under the warmth of the sun as the scent of the sea surrounds us in an embrace feels like the moment my mother always described.

You are exactly where you're meant to be when you're meant to be there doing what you're meant to do.

Whether reincarnation is real or not, we'll never know, but what I do know is that I can't explain what happened here. Maybe I don't need to. Maybe instead of explaining, it's meant only to exist as it is - a voice shouting out into the chasm of eternity begging to be heard. If I've learned anything about love recently, it's that it's the only thing that survives when we do not. It's what keeps history alive, and I feel so lucky right now to understand exactly why.

With a kiss to end all kisses, Theo pulls us toward the flower shop where he chooses a bouquet for Mom, and I choose him for the rest of my life.

Chapter Thirty-Three

Theodore

Dessa's mother hasn't stopped hugging me, and I can already see where Dessa inherited her strength from. Becca, as she insisted I call her, is a creative powerhouse from what I understand, and has been a guiding light to Dessa her entire life. Finally seeing Becca and David together and how they interact, it makes perfect sense as to how Dessa cares for other people. She wants what her parents have, and she loves with her whole heart. I couldn't have hoped for a more beautiful soul to fall for.

"Will you two join us for dinner later? We're going to head back and spend some time together," David says, and Becca winks at Dessa who rolls her eyes playfully at the thought of her parents being romantic. "I have a lot to fill her in on."

"Thank you for inviting me. That's so kind of you," I add. "I'd really love to."

"You don't have to be so formal with us, sweetheart. You clearly love my daughter. You're in the family now whether you like it or not," Becca admits with a smile as David wraps an arm around her shoulders, and I lace my fingers with Dessa's.

It really does feel like I'm part of her family, part of *her*. When I look down at her, she's beaming up at me with a smile that shines brightly in her eyes even from behind her glasses. The sense of belonging is new to me, but I could get very used to having family in the States. I could get very used to having her as my family wherever I go.

"Yup, you're one of us now," Dessa says softly to me with a smile that makes me want to kiss her for hours. "You ok with that?"

"If it means I get to keep you, then a thousand times yes," I whisper to her with a kiss on her head. I watch her mother melt and her father beam knowing that I am utterly smitten and hopelessly in love with their daughter. My mum always said the moment you want to quote classic literature just from looking at a girl, that's when you know you're in love. And she's right. One look at Dessa and I understand every poet, every artist, and every musician influenced by their hearts.

Watching as David and Becca walk down the dock to board their boat, all I can see is the future I never knew I needed. Now that I've seen what my life could look like, I don't want anything else. Looking down at her, my email notification goes off and I pull my phone from my pocket without letting her go. We both see the preview message at the same time - the final payment from the Goodmans for the appraisals.

"Aside from your dashing accent, I almost forgot you were just here on business," Dessa says with a slight tinge of sadness in her tone. She wraps her arms around my waist and pouts, and I don't care how old she gets, that will work on me for the remainder of my time on this planet.

"I talked to the bed & breakfast to stay a few more days before I fly back," I reveal, having extended my stay the moment I knew she loved me back. "I'd like it if you stayed with me there."

"I would love to...and I'm sure my parents would appreciate the time together after everything," she admits. I try to focus on her words, but the idea of staying lazily tangled in my sheets with her for three entire days has my mind racing with everything I want to feel with her.

"I want the time together too," I laugh, nuzzling her neck and kissing her jaw when an idea strikes. "I'm supposed to stop by their house to sign a few last minute things. Come with me."

She nods without saying a word, the tickle of her chestnut waves on my face giving me flashbacks of the intimate night we spent together. As we turn to walk together, something feels important to remind her of.

"You know, Nora and Henry might not have been the original lovers," I suggest as we make our way to the Goodman's place. It's only about a ten minute walk, but it feels shorter when the weather is good. She looks up at me, her brow raised in curiosity. "Maybe we come from a long line."

"I think even if we didn't, I would have fallen for you all the same," she admits freely and willingly, just as I had planned too.

"Me too, my light. Me too," I agree and squeeze her hand. "England is beautiful this time of year too, and I know Mum and Greta would love to meet you...especially since they know everything about you already."

"I've always wanted to visit," she says with a smile. "And I would love to meet them too...maybe I could see them as soon as I submit my project and finish helping with the house. Is that ok? It might be a week or two."

"Then I say it's a date, love. Not even time can separate us anymore," I reply genuinely just to watch her glow at the adoration.

Stopping in the middle of the sidewalk, I pull her in and tilt her chin up for a kiss I don't hesitate to deepen regardless of whether or not we're being watched by the locals. I don't want to ever stop kissing her. As her hold on me tightens, and we're lost in each other, a small breeze curls around us carrying a scent that is reminiscent of lavender and the sea. Just as fast as it appears, it is gone - a faint hello from a place we've never been but know exists. Pulling my lips away from hers just to make it to the Goodman's on time was the hardest thing I've had to do since I arrived in this town. Dusting a kiss to her forehead, I lace my hand in hers, and lead her through the picket fence's gate to the front door.

The moment we cross over the welcome mat, Sarah wraps her arms around Dessa like an old friend and leads us to the floral couch. The coffee table is set for afternoon tea, and the house carries the scent of morning warmth and familial comfort. It makes me miss my mum and sister even more, although they've thoroughly enjoyed all of my updates and are beyond thrilled to meet Dessa. It's only June and she's already started to talk of winter plans and taking her shopping at all the Christmas markets, convinced the holidays are more festive in England.

"I'm so glad you were both able to visit before you're back off across the pond as you say," Sarah says with an attempt at an accent, all of us breaking out into a giggle at it. "You really have helped us so much, dear, and the things we've listed for sale are going to afford us more than we'd hoped for. And you know how happy you've made Stanford. He hasn't stopped gushing about the donations for his little museum."

"Of course," I reply with a gracious nod of my head. It's always hard to accept thanks for a job I'm being paid for, but it's also something I genuinely love to do, so I am lucky in that right as well. "I'm so happy for you both, and of course for Stan."

"And you, my dear?" Sarah asks, directing her attention to Odessa, and leaning over the coffee table from her arm chair to place a wrinkled hand on top of hers. "Corlucius Island is a treasure in and of itself. Has it spoken to you yet? Has it given you its secrets?" She carries a look in her eyes that makes me believe she knows so much more than she's telling us, but it's also one of sympathy, as if she's carried something on her conscience until now.

"Corlucius doesn't tell its secrets," Dessa whispers, almost as if there were people closeby she doesn't want to hear. "She sings them." As soon as the words leave her lips, Sarah's eyes well up with tears, and she nods with a smile. I wonder how much Sarah knows, and if that knowledge is derived from passed down oral history in her family, or if she's been tuned into a channel we've only just discovered.

"Yes, darling," Sarah says with a knowing nod. "Yes, she does." The two share a wordless exchange, communicating only by the soft smiles they wear and the way their hands rest together. When the brief moment passes, Sarah sits up and takes a deep breath as if to clear the board when the tea kettle whistles from the kitchen. "Would you be a dear and bring the tea, Odessa?"

"My pleasure," she agrees with a nod and walks into the kitchen. The moment Dessa is out of the room, Sarah turns to me as if she has something she'd like to say.

"There's one more item for you, child," she says with a hushed tone as my curiosity piques. "It's been in my family for almost as long as we've lived here, but as you know, a found item does not mean it's yours. We've held it for generations, but it never fit. The promise we've made to it is that we'd know when it was time to give it away. We'd know who it was meant to belong to when it told us."

"What do you mean?" I ask, leaning forward from the couch to catch the first glimpse of whatever she just pulled from the pocket of her light blue cardigan.

It's small and whatever it is she's holding, it's wrapped delicately in a handkerchief. As soon as she puts it in my hands, my entire body is wrapped in a warm wave. Similar to the feeling I had when the compass touched my palm, I feel it again but with an intensity I've never known. Whatever it is, it feels like mine, but before I can open it, she puts her hand over mine and the small package.

"My family has owned various shops and things here on the mainland, and they've collected some interesting things. Some from estate sales or trades, and some were salvaged off the shore in unfortunate times...like shipwrecks."

The words pull something inside me I can't explain, a chord in my heart of knowing - one that feels seen in a moment of screaming out into a dark void. With a gentle nod, she moves her hand away from mine to let me unfold the small package corner by corner. The moment the final corner is opened like a slowly blooming night flower, I sharply inhale.

"You found it," I say without hesitation or understanding. In my hands, gently resting in the center of the white handkerchief is a small gold ring. Picking up the delicate trinket, I feel an ecstatic sense of joy and love. I can't explain how I know it's mine, but I think we've far passed the point of needing to define that which defies all logic and reason. And perhaps the moment you know is the moment you decide you don't need to know. Perhaps you just exist in the moment as it presents itself and that's all you need.

"It's about time you got it back, my dear," Sarah says with a beaming smile and I return it from ear to ear, carefully folding the corners back into place, putting the ring into my pocket just in time for Dessa to return with our tea.

***

Spending three days wrapped in each other was the closest I've ever known to heaven on earth. I lost count of the times we kissed, tasted each other, or made love. Her body is an art gallery I could spend lifetimes exploring. The starry night of her eyes, the sunflowers of her smile, the water lilies of her lips. I could stare and admire the way the universe's brushstrokes created the curve of her hips or the delicate line from her neck to her shoulders. She is art incarnate and I'm lucky to be standing in front of her just to watch the moment the warm glow of the sunset makes the gold flecks in her pupils shine. My Helen of Troy. My Evie from The Mummy. My light.

After the incessant texts and calls we were both getting from our friends and family, we spent one of those afternoons on countless Facetimes and Zooms to introduce each other to those we love the most. Mum and Greta were beyond thrilled to not only see and hear Dessa on the screen, but to see what I look like when I'm the happiest I've ever been in my life. When it was just Mum and I on the line, I told her my plans to make Dessa my wife, and she told me it's all she's ever wanted for me. Greta, who was eavesdropping as she always has, cheered at the promise of a sister and claimed I was even more outnumbered in the family now. Dessa's best friends, Aly and Savannah, were tough on the first call, but after dealing with someone like Marcus, of course they want their best friend to be happy and safe.

I can see now how lucky I am to be included in her lives, and loved by the people that love her.

As we walk out of McNamara's after lunch on my last day, we keep our fingers laced and the way my body reacts to the small squeeze she gives my hand in appreciation could power a thousand cities. It's going to be a tough adjustment to go from having each other all day for every meal to Facetimes and calls until we book another flight. Although it hasn't been years of courtship, in the infinite span of time, we're only a blink, and a blink is all it would take to miss the chance to touch her or be the reason her cheeks flush.

"Keep looking at me like that, Indiana Jones, and I'm not going to let you board that plane," she says with a smile before I realize I've been staring. I chuckle at the nicknames we've given each other for our favorite fictional archeologists.

"I don't think that sounds so bad, Evie," I return and she blushes.

"Your mother would revoke my invitation," she laughs, and I know she's right. Mum has missed me so much, we're all sick of hearing about it. "But as soon as the house is done, then I'm all yours."

"I like the sound of that. All mine," I say holding her as we stop to stand near the dock overlooking the water. "I love you in this lifetime and every other."

"I love you, and I'm yours in every single one," she replies as I pull her in for a kiss that I'll regret having to end. When I pull back, I smile at the way her cheeks flush, and it reminds me of every way I've made her blush in the past few days in every place we could. As if she can see the way the flashbacks of our intimacy affect me, she smiles playfully. "You could always come visit me this summer while we're working on the house. Just a surprise visit perhaps?"

"Mmmm," I pretend to ponder as I hold her tighter. "If I surprise you, how will I know you're home?"

"I'll leave the light on," she says with a look that tells me our future was built from lifetimes of love, letters of longing, and just a touch of magic.

The End

ONE YEAR LATER

DESTINATION RENOVATION - EPISODE 13

Transcript: Closed Captioning

Intro Music - Fade in and Fade Out - Original Theme Song "Roads of Love" by Jack Jack

Becca: Hey everyone and welcome back to our show. I'm Becca -

David: And I'm Dave-

Becca: - and this is Destination Restoration part 13, well I guess it's not exactly a part. It's more of an update episode. For those of you who are just now joining us after the Netflix special, welcome and we hope you stick around. We're going to do a bit of a recap for the curious newcomers, so if you've been with us for the whole Corlucius series, thank you and you can skip to the next part or jump around by clicking the timestamps in the description. Whatever the reason, thank you for joining us today as we do our final updates on the Corlucius Island property.

Transition - Montage & Music - 8 seconds - "Corlucius Island Recap" Title Page

David: A year and a half ago we'd just completed the Hammond House, and we decided that when we were ready for the next project we'd know. Becks and I had a great time with you all on that house, but you know how it goes when you do a hobby like it's a job, then it feels like work and not like fun.

Becca: So, I told him that when the next project wanted to be found, it would show itself to us. My mom had a little saying that I use and I passed it down to my daughter. She would say, "if you're ever unsure or confused, just remember, you're exactly where you're meant to be when you're meant to be there doing what you're meant to do". And sure enough that's how Corlucius found us.

David: We'd just watched a documentary about the most unique historical landmarks around the country, so I thought that it would be interesting to try that type of restoration next.

Becca: What he didn't realize is that when he said we'd try it next, I was already scrolling through listings next to him.

David: That's because someone doesn't like to just sit still.

Becca: Because I'm like the wind, baby.

David: So Miss Windy over here found a couple of listings for historical homes and sites, and we toured one or two, but they just didn't give us that feeling.

Becca: We need that feeling to choose a restoration project because you have to be in love with it if you're going to spend every waking second there for months. We decided to stop looking and wait for a project to find us organically. You know how it is ladies, you stop looking for Mr. Right and he appears when you least expect it.

David: And this property was definitely unexpected. We were walking around a vintage flea market because there's no way Becks can pass one of those up. It was one of those ones where there's all kinds of tables of old trinkets, flowers, crafts, you name it - it's there. So we're walking around just looking, well I'm looking, she's buying everything.

Becca: I can't help that I have an eye for it. But I'm looking around at this one table, and I see a small snow globe. It's a little lighthouse and it's stunning. At the bottom, there was a location scratched off, and I couldn't tell where it was from, so I bought it and did some research.

David: Because she loves mysteries.

Becca: I absolutely do. So I look into this lighthouse, and I narrowed it down to three. It turns out it was the Boston Light, but in my search I found Corlucius Island and the lighthouse. The more I read about it, the more I fell in love with it. Plus, I'd learned that the previous owner meant to renovate it, but took a job offer elsewhere. We decided to fly out to Massachusetts to take a tour, and that was it. It just felt like ours. It's the only way I know how to explain it.

David: Within weeks, we'd gone to a tour, placed an offer, it was accepted, and we closed. Moving to New England from SoCal was an adventure, and we fell in love with living here too. We ended up getting in a little deeper than we'd anticipated with all the things that needed fixed, including the wiring for the beacon itself. It definitely pushed my skillset and I had to get out of my comfort zone to make it happen.

Becca: And he did so much of it while I was hospitalized during the reno. Which is a reminder again to please remember your PPE, and always wear a mask when you're getting into these older homes and projects. The mold and dust is no joke.

Dave: Our daughter, Odessa, flew out as well so we had a lot of help and we really enjoyed bringing this property back to life to its former glory. Let's take a look at some of the behind the scenes footage of our reno now.

Transition - Video Footage Montage of Reno - 32 minutes

Becca: And now for the update portion of our episode...

Dave: We have decided not to keep the property. It's too important to the residents, the generations of the people before them, and all of the lighthouse keepers. It's something we felt very strongly about after everything that happened, and although most of the other things are purely speculation, we made the decision because we felt that the community deserved to have a pivotal piece of its history back.

Becca: A few things to add to that for you viewers, is that we have donated the property to the city and its historical society and Maritime Museum, so it will never need new owners, and it'll be maintained well by the people that have loved it for generations. From what we understand, they plan to turn the property into a museum of sorts, and right now they're working on a stone monument to honor the sacrifice of all previous lighthouse keepers.

Dave: Stay tuned on that front because they also told us that once that's finished, they'll be celebrating it's history annually when the mainland celebrates it's July birthday. Watch their website for more details, we'll link it below, and maybe one day you'll be able to visit Corlucius Island too.

Becca: In the meantime, all of your comments were correct. We are going to stay, just not on the island. We got a pretty good deal on a house after we donated the property, and we made a lot of great friends in the community who appreciate the island returning back to proper ownership. Yes, I love the Corlucius Lighthouse, but now we can look at it every night from our new home. There's a great view out of the loft window. Let's take a look.

Transition - Loft Footage - 7 minutes

Dave: And to wrap up our recap episode, we know you're all waiting very patiently (or not so patiently if you just skipped chapters) for the paranormal update.

Becca: Because who wouldn't love a story about ghosts in a haunted lighthouse, right?

Dave: I can't confirm everything in the Netflix special that aired, and you know how these things are when they say they're based on actual or true events. The important word to remember is "based" though, so it doesn't make every single thing you saw in that special true.

Becca: There have been no reports of paranormal activity in the past almost year, but we like to think it's because they don't have to fight to be seen anymore. With a museum to honor them all, they're not only seen, but learned about and heard every day with new tour groups and class field trips. Maybe you'll go there and feel a hand on your shoulder, or maybe you'll hear a whistled tune, or smell tobacco, but other than that, there are no ghosts left suffering at Corlucius Island.

Dave: And if it's the paranormal you like, then really it's the history you love, so when you visit the mainland and you're waiting for the ferry, please stop by the Maritime Museum and Historical Society located inside the library. There's a lot of information and artifacts you won't find anywhere else.

Becca: And also while you're there, please stop into The Broken Mast, it's an amazing restaurant.

Dave: Tell them why, honey.

Becca: They'll see it.

Dave: *laughs* If you read the menu for The Broken Mast, there's a lunch special they've named after us for donating the property, and someone insists on having it every week.

Becca: You should all try it and you'll understand why I order it every week. The namesake is a total bonus.

Dave: Sure it is...

Becca: *laughs* Ok fine, it makes me feel a little starstruck and I also really love it.

Dave: That's all we have for you in this update episode, so stay tuned and we'll be live streaming the first birthday celebration from the island and hosting the lighting of the fireworks and ribbon cutting.

Becca: We're excited to see you there! If you're there in person, come say hi and give us a hug! If you're with us online, drop those locations in the comments so we can see how far the light reaches.

Dave: See you then!

Becca: And thanks for joining us on another season of...

Dave and Becca (together): Destination Restoration!

Becca: Stay tuned for bloopers after the credits and thank you's! See you next time!

Outro Music - Fade in and Fade Out - Original Theme Song "Roads of Love" by Jack Jack

FIVE YEARS LATER

ODESSA

"There he is!" Mom's voice sounds just beyond the dock as Theo reaches the rope to tie us to the metal hooks. Thomas is already so excited to see her that he's jumping up and down causing his little light-up shoes to strobe and flash in reds, blues, and greens. As his excitement rocks the small boat a little, I smile with a hand over my swollen belly at the manifestation of his joy.

"Be careful, son, we don't want to shake your mum and your little sister, do we?" Theo says gently to Thomas as they both look at me with matching smiles, and I can see how thrilled they are to bring another part of our family into the world.

As the boat is secured, Theo steps onto the dock first to steady it and reaches for Thomas, who practically flies out of the small ferry and races down the dock to the sound of my Mom and Dad calling to their favorite (and only) grandson. With a small shake of the head shared between my husband and I, he holds his hand out to me and I oblige, letting him pull me and our future daughter into his body on the dock.

"Be careful there, Mrs. Montgomery," he says playfully as he brushes one of my chocolate curls out of my eyes and behind my ear, tucking it under the arm of my tortoise shell glasses. His eyes in the late afternoon sun beam with adoration and reverence, making me flush with the spark that his gaze still ignites within me.

"Well, Mr. Montgomery, it's not like I can get pregnant," I tease, knowing the way he's holding me is precisely how our little girl came to be unexpectedly. He brings me in a little tighter to slide his hand from my ear to the base of my head, his fingers raking through my hair and I close my eyes at the tender touch. Kissing the crown of my head, he lingers there for a moment as I wrap my arms around him as best I can.

"It feels different coming back here now, doesn't it?" Theo asks into my hair before pulling back to see my face and steal a kiss as I nod. "We'd better be off to find Thomas then. Let's see what they've done to the place, yes?"

"I'm sure he's already prepared to become a tour guide for this evening," I laugh. Our little Thomas is a never ending spout of fun facts and trivia as he spends all of his time with us at work, with his grandparents, and watching documentaries. Currently, he's been very interested in ships, so he's excited to visit the Maritime Museum tomorrow.

Walking up the new wooden stairs to the island's edge, the Corlucius Lighthouse and keeper's house come into view, as well as the vision of people walking all over the grounds with clipboards and cameras. The highly anticipated annual birthday celebration is still hours away, but it's the biggest event of the year, so the pressure to make it successful feels palpable in the atmosphere. Theo's fingers stay laced with mine as we look at each other and smile, the memories of this place reminding us of destiny, fate, and magic coexisting with the unaware mortal world.

Looking back and forth to search for my parents and Thomas, we walk toward the house as Theo rubs circles with his thumb on the back of my palm. He likes to keep checking in with me in every little way even before I was carrying our daughter, and now he's so excited, it's more than common.

"Thomas!" Theo calls, not out of fear, but out of ensuring I'm not on my feet longer than necessary to look for him all over the island. At least he can't wander far on an island.

"Over here, Dad!" a small voice calls to the left of the keeper's house and we follow with shared creased brows at what has captured his interest.

Holding a hand over my eyes in the warm sun, we walk toward the sound. As soon as we see him, we smile. He's standing under the tree almost as if he's whispering behind the thick trunk of it.

"What are you doing over here, sweetheart?" I ask. His face is so curious and bright with the small gap on the bottom from his first lost tooth still one of the most adorable things I've ever seen in my life.

"Mom, I was talking to this nice lady," Thomas says looking back and forth like he lost something dear to him. Theo and I shared a confused look and share his search, looking around the grounds for the woman Thomas was speaking to. All I see are a few men wearing headsets and utility belts with matching t-shirts from what I'm sure is the company they've hired to setoff the fireworks.

"What nice lady, Thomas?" Theo asks, sharing my confusion. Thomas places one hand on the trunk of the tree and begins to run in a circle around it, using his hand to keep his balance.

"Umm she's pretty," Thomas starts as he runs two laps around the tree and continues. "She says she remembers you." Another lap. "And you." Another lap. "Who is she, Mommy?"

Placing a hand over my belly, I glance at Theo with a soft smile who is already looking at me with an expression that tells me we're thinking the same thing. We are long past pretending that ghosts aren't part of our lives. They're everywhere around us and live in every piece of art, architecture, or story. They're living libraries of the past, and if we're lucky, they can guide us to each other.

"She's our friend," Theo says gently as he takes my hand.

"She looks like a angel," Thomas says, his light-up shoes still blinking brightly with every circle he runs around the tree.

"That's because she is, my darling," I tell him, and I swear I can feel the gratitude of recognition in air. When I hear my mother's voice call out to Thomas again, he waves at us and runs off toward the keeper's house where I know he'll find chocolate chip cookies and his favorite juice box flavors.

As Theo and I are left under the tree, with one hand over our daughter and the other laced in love, we share a silent moment for everything that's happened in all of time for us to be standing in this very spot. Without a word, we take our joined hands and move them to the tree trunk, flattening my palm against the bark and his on top of mine. Breathing in and out, we close our eyes for just a moment.

As if the veil thinned just for us, a gentle breeze dances through the leaves and part the branches ever so slightly to allow one bright, warm beam of sun to bathe the three of us in a brief beautiful glow that feels like a hug. Theo moves his other hand on top of mine resting on my belly. In a soft moment, the world stills and it's only us here in the late afternoon sun. Softly leaning forward, I touch my lips to the bark to kiss the past.

"We're naming her Abigail," I whisper for no one else to hear but the ghosts. It's a name I fell in love with when we did the full research for my masters program and the island's memorial to the previous keepers. Eleanor, Phillip, and Abigail Shoemaker were the original keepers, and the moment I saw her name, we knew it would belong to us if we ever had a daughter.

As I whisper the words, Theo kisses me on the head and my vintage ring catches in the light making it shine like new. Every time it shines, I remember the perfect memories we've made so far. His proposal. Our wedding. Our son. It's the life of love I've always dreamed of with the man the universe dreamed for me.

When darkness finally blankets the shore and sea, we get our places ready to see the birthday celebration fireworks show. Thomas is already yawning, especially after eating his weight in my dad's burnt hamburgers. Mom is still fawning over me, making sure I'm keeping her future granddaughter comfortable and well fed. If I eat one more burger, I'm going to pop out of this dress. Dad is lifting Thomas to his shoulders, as the crew gets ready to light the first firework section for the show.

Theo and I stand together with my back to his front and his arms under my belly to support the weight and give me a break. Leaning my head back at the blissful release, we sway as he whispers in my ear, his stubble scratching my cheek and making me blush at the tickle.

"I love you, Dessa. In every form. In every lifetime. In every version of us that has ever existed," he says softly, speaking the words into my skin with devotion and reverence. No matter how many times I hear our wedding vows, I'll never tire of them.

"And I love you dearly, my Theodore. In every form. In every lifetime. In every version of us that has ever existed," I return back to him. Whether reincarnation is real or not, I know with all certainty that my soul is connected to his, and destiny will always intervene to help us find each other like a beacon in the dark.

As Thomas claps and cheers for the start of the fireworks show, the installed lights around the property flare to life, illuminating the lighthouse and keeper's house. Cheers can be heard all around us as the display in the sky shimmers and sparkles and pops. Feeling an unexplained nudge to look away from the sky's show, Theo and I turn to glance back at the keeper's house.

In the small window that once belonged to me, and to Eleanor long before that, a small candle ignites. Before Theo or I can say a word, we both register a small kick from little Abigail. It's the first kick, and as we tear up, the flame in the window burns bright.

"I guess some things never change," I say with a knowing smile to the love of every lifetime as his arms hold me tighter.

"And love will always light the way," he answers and brings me to his lips for a kiss under the shimmering fireworks of Corlucius Island.

AFTERWORD

I've loved lighthouses and maritime history for a long time. Growing up on the east coast allowed me to spend summer vacations experiencing the climb to the top of the Hatteras Lighthouse in North Carolina and heading out onto the Chesapeake Bay to try my hand at laying crab pots and dredging for oysters. As most people my age, I was also obsessed with the Titanic and other shipwrecks.

This story came to me in a dream over ten years ago, and I didn't know how I wanted to write it, so I let it slip to the back of my mind. I kept telling myself that when the time was right to write it, I would know. Oddly enough, little signs started pushing me to the right direction and as I was describing them to a friend, she said something that gave me a slight chill in the best way. In all seriousness, she said, "some people just want their story to be told". That's how I envision this book – a story that wants to be told.

I also wanted to share the meaning behind the names I chose to add another layer of understanding to the story.

- Eleanor means "light" or "shining light"

- Odessa means "journey"

- Corlucius means "heart" and "light"

Acknowledgements

This story has been on the back burner longer than any other book idea I've ever had. I'd like to give a huge thank you to anyone that's suffered through listening to me work this plot out through email, text, voice memo, in person, or on the phone.

Thank you to the people in my life who have cheered me on throughout this book, and the rest of my author journey that I've only just begun. It consumes a lot of my time, thought, and energy, so I greatly appreciate the people that support me through the process of passing thought to completed project. You are the real MVPs!

Thank you to my fellow indie authors that have answered my non-stop texts (and countless versions of a blurb I struggled to nail down), sent me Tiktoks, tagged me in posts to help my books, and more. You know who you are, but in case you need a reminder – thank you forever to Melissa, Sienna, Sarah, and Jessica!

And thank you to YOU, the readers who read beta, arc, and final copies of this book. It means the entire world to me that you chose to give my characters (and me) a chance. When I was a kid, I wanted to be a writer, and when you show up at events and read my books, it shows her that we made it through ok. You help me make her proud, and I can't thank you enough for that. It's pure magic.

About the Author

A lifetime avid reader, India has always dreamed of bringing her own stories to the world, doing so with her debut novel "Alligator Blood". When she's not busy working or on an adventure (either in person or in a Dungeon & Dragons campaign), you can find her on the couch cuddled up in her Ghostface fleece blanket watching disturbing horror movie marathons and eating enough snacks for an entire kindergarten class.

Follow for updates, memes, and chaos:
Tiktok: @Indiavanebooks
Instagram: @Indiavanebooks

ALSO BY

INDIA VANE

Standalones:

Alligator Blood – spicy suspense
Leave the Light On – paranormal romance

Bright Ridge Six Series:

Inked Magnolia – contemporary romance